The Riddle of the Rajah's Ruby

Enid Blyton

The Riddle of the Rajah's Ruby

AWARD PUBLICATIONS LIMITED

This book was first published in Great Britain
under the title *The Adventure of the Strange Ruby* by
The Brockhampton Press in 1960. It was updated and
altered to become part of the Riddle series in 1997
by Enid Blyton's daughter, Gillian Baverstock.

For further information on Enid Blyton
please visit *www.blyton.com*

ISBN 978-1-84135-739-3

Illustrated by Patricia Ludlow
Cover illustration by Gavin Rowe

First published 1960 as *The Adventure of the Strange Ruby*
Revised edition published 1997 as *The Riddle of the Rajah's Ruby*
First published by Award Publications Limited 2004 as
The Young Adventurers and the Rajah's Ruby
This edition entitled *The Riddle of the Rajah's Ruby*
first published 2009

Published by Award Publications Limited,
The Old Riding School, The Welbeck Estate,
Worksop, Nottinghamshire, S80 3LR

12 3

Printed in the United Kingdom

CONTENTS

CHAPTER 1

A LITTLE BIT OF NEWS

It all began when Nick Terry picked up the paper one morning and read a little paragraph tucked away in a corner.

He was first down for breakfast. Not even his father was there yet, so Nick was able to have a look at the paper first. That didn't often happen.

The headlines weren't interesting, something about mortgage rates rising again, whatever that meant. Nick's eyes slid down the page and came to four small paragraphs. They were headed THE RAJAH'S RUBY.

He read the paragraphs and then read them again. He was just finishing when he heard footsteps coming down the stairs, and his sister Katie burst into the room with Punch, their black and white terrier, racing after her.

"Phew! I thought I was late," she said in relief. "Isn't Dad down yet?"

"No. I bet he's lost his socks again," said Nick. "I've heard a lot of scrambling going on upstairs. But Katie, look what's in the paper."

Katie took the paper and read the paragraph out loud.

THE RAJAH'S RUBY

This sinister ruby, the biggest in the world, is once more in the news. For centuries it gleamed in the head of a great statue in a temple on an Indian hillside, one of a pair of enormous ruby eyes.

During a tribal war both rubies were stolen. One was never heard of again. The other eventually found its way into the hands of a powerful Indian ruler who, in return for the saving of his life, gave it to an Englishman, Major Ellis Gathergood.

He died suddenly and the ruby passed to another member of the family. But misfortune continually followed the owners of the ruby, and one member of the Gathergood family let it be known that he had sold the Rajah's Ruby. It has certainly never been heard of to this day.

It was, however, always believed to be

in the possession of Mrs Eleanor Gathergood, who has just died. If so, the sinister ruby will pass to her nearest relatives, twelve-year-old twins Sophie and David Gathergood. What will they do with it?

Katie looked up at Nick in excitement.

"Why, those are the twins we met at Swanage last year! I stayed with Sophie after our holiday finished because David went camping, do you remember? They must be twelve now – a year older than you and two years older than me. We had a lot of fun with them. I'll never forget the night we all went mackerel fishing and Sophie felt so sorry for the fish she wouldn't come again!"

"No, nor will I! And remember the day David nearly capsized the sailing boat and poor Punch fell overboard so David had to dive in and rescue him? We had really good fun together," said Nick. "They had a sort of nanny, didn't they? We were sorry for them because they hadn't any parents – only a great-aunt or someone like that."

"She's the Mrs Eleanor Gathergood who has just died," said Katie. "I met her when I stayed there. She was a dear old lady but she couldn't do much because she had a bad heart."

"Have you still got their address, Katie?" asked Nick. "Let's write and ask them if they really do own the Rajah's Ruby. They might show it to us!"

"I bet they wouldn't be allowed to have it on show," said Katie. "But we ought to write to them anyway to say we're sorry old Mrs Gathergood is dead."

"It says, 'Misfortune has continually followed the owners of the ruby'," said Nick, looking at the paper again. "I hope bad luck doesn't come to David and Sophie – they've had quite enough already."

"Yes, they have. Their mother dying when they were born, and their father being killed in an accident is enough bad luck to last them for the rest of their lives," said Katie. "Hello, here's Dad at last. Stop barking, Punch. You know Dad hates noise at breakfast."

Mr Terry came into the room and was welcomed by Punch jumping up at him and trying to lick his hands. "Get down, Punch," he shouted. "I really won't have you in the room while we're eating, if you can't behave!" He looked surprised to see Katie and Nick down first. "Turning over a new leaf?" he asked and picked up the paper. "Didn't you know the hall clock was fast?"

"Oh no!" said Nick, pushing Punch

under the table. "I simply leaped out of bed when I heard it strike eight. I bet you put it fast on purpose, Dad, because we were so late yesterday."

"I wouldn't be surprised!" said their mother, coming in. "Get back under the table, Punch, and be quiet." She sat down at the end of the table. "Well, any news in the paper?"

Nick told her about the piece he had read, and she nodded. "Yes, those *are* the twins we met last year. And now I come to think of it, the woman who looked after them said she was upset because their great-aunt was ill, and she was afraid that if she died, that ruby might be left to the twins. I remember I was horrified to hear her say that if it was, she would leave them at once, because she was afraid she might share in any bad luck that came to them through the ruby."

"What nonsense!" said her husband.

"I did like Sophie and David," said Katie. "I've still got their address some-where. We're going to write and ask them if they own the ruby now, Mum."

"They probably won't be told," said Mrs

Terry, pouring out the tea. "I was sorry for those children, they seemed so completely on their own with no parents, no aunts or uncles or cousins. I was glad you made friends with them. They were both very striking-looking with their curly red hair and vivid blue eyes."

"It must be dreadful to be orphans like that," said Katie. "I couldn't bear it if anything happened to you and Dad."

"We'll take great care of ourselves, I promise you!" said her mother with a smile. "Now, Gran's not feeling very well this morning and she'd just like a cup of tea and a slice of toast and marmalade. You've nearly finished, Katie, would you lay a tray for her and take it up, please?"

"Poor Gran! This is my last mouthful so I'll go and do it now," said Katie, and she went off to the kitchen.

After breakfast, Nick and Katie went upstairs and rummaged about in their desks. As usual they were in a terrible muddle. It was a wonder they ever found anything they wanted. Punch thought he was helping by searching in the corners of the room, but as he only found a chewed slipper, a pencil case, a dirty sweater and a ball, he wasn't much use!

Katie at last found what she was looking for. She pulled out an old notebook and flourished it.

"Here's my address book. I haven't seen it since I was sending Christmas cards last December. Now I'll look for the twins' address."

She flipped over the pages and then came to a stop. "Here it is, but I can hardly read my own writing! I think it says David and Sophie Gathergood, Hailey House, Tipscombe, Wilts. Let's write today."

"All right, but you do the letter," said Nick, who never wrote to anyone if he could help it. "Anyway, you know Sophie much better than I do, from staying with her."

So Katie wrote the letter – and that is how it was that she and Nick came to share in the extraordinary adventure of the Rajah's Ruby.

CHAPTER 2

Two Interesting Letters

No answer came to Katie's letter for some time. "I expect it had to be forwarded from their home address to their school," said Katie. "They go to boarding school, don't they, not to day school, like us."

In July, Gran went away to stay with an old friend for six weeks. "I need a bit of peace and quiet while you're home for the summer," she said. "I shall miss you all, even that noisy dog who takes my slippers away and puts them where I can't find them! Have a lovely time in Swanage and make sure you help your mother. Don't let her do everything."

The end of term came, and still there was no answer from the twins. Then, on the third day of the summer holidays, a letter came addressed to Katie. It was from Sophie.

"Now we'll hear their news," said Katie,

tearing open the envelope. Nick came and looked over her shoulder. They read in silence.

Dear Katie and Nick,

Thanks for your letter. It was fantastic to hear from you again. Yes, it was our great-aunt who died. We were rich before, and now I suppose we're richer, which is a real nuisance, because what we really want to do when we're older is just to run a riding stables, and you don't need millions of pounds for that. At least, if you do, you can earn it, and that's fun. Just having money left to you is no fun at all.

And we've got the ruby – at least, it's being kept for us, though we don't want anything to do with the beastly jewel. We haven't even seen it.

Do you remember Miss Lawley, who looked after us? Well, she's gone. She's afraid of the ruby! Can you imagine anything so idiotic – afraid of a red stone! She told us awful things about it before she went, trying to scare us, but you know David and me, we just laughed at her.

We're having someone else soon, I don't

*know who. Someone pathetic, I expect –
couldn't be worse than old Lawley,
anyway, with her scare-stories!*

*We're going away somewhere for the
hols. I don't know where, because for some
reason or other it's all hush-hush. If only
it was Swanage again! If we can manage
to find out where we're going, we'll send a
note. David sends you one of his grins.*

Love from
Sophie

Katie looked at Nick. "So that woman kept
her word! She couldn't have been very fond
of them. It must be pretty awful to have
nobody who loves you, no mother or
anything."

"Well, they've got each other, and you
know what twins are," said Nick. "They
stick together like glue, usually. I do hope
they'll manage to let us know where they're
going for a holiday. I only wish it was
somewhere near us."

They heard nothing more for a whole
week, and then another letter turned up,
rather grubby and creased, which held only
a few lines:

Dear Katie and Nick

*Only have a moment to scribble this –
we're going off somewhere now, this
minute, in a car. Things aren't too good,
somehow. All we know is that we
overheard someone mention Bringking
Hill – at least that's what it sounded like.
We're throwing this letter out of the car,
hoping it will be found and posted by
someone. We'll write again if we can.*

Sophie

Nick and Katie read this twice. Then they
looked at one another.

"What does Sophie mean by 'things
aren't too good, somehow', do you
suppose?" said Nick. "And why weren't they
told where they were going? They must
have asked! And why on earth weren't they
allowed even to post a letter?"

"It does seem rather peculiar," said
Katie. "But of course the twins always were
a bit mad, and given to making mysteries
out of things, weren't they? We'll probably
get a letter or card in a day or two with
their proper address."

But they didn't. No letter or card came at

all. Then for some reason Katie began to worry.

"I'm sure there's something up," she said. "I've got one of my feelings. I think we ought to tell Mum."

"Don't be so silly," said Nick. "You and your feelings! The last time you had a feeling it was about Dumpy the cat, and you gave me an awful time making me think she had been run over and killed or something – and she was in the kitchen all the time."

"But she had stolen all that fish left out ready for our dinner," said Katie. "And my feeling about Punch was spot on when he got locked in the garage!"

"If you're going to have feelings about cats stealing fish, I don't think much of them," said Nick. "As for your feeling about Punch – you heard him barking frantically!"

"I did not!" said Katie, indignantly. "I had a feeling about him and so I went to look for him and when I went into the garden I heard him barking in the garage, so there!"

"Okay, okay! Look, I'll tell you what

we'll do about the twins, Katie – we'll look in Dad's road atlas, the one that gives all the towns of Britain, and see if Bringking Hill is mentioned."

There was no mention of Bringking Hill, but there was apparently a village called Brinkin and, what was more, it was in Dorset, not so very far from Swanage where the children had gone on holiday for several years.

"Hey, suppose this Brinkin is the Bringking Hill Sophie mentioned!" said Nick. "We're going down to Swanage soon and we might be able to find Brinkin Hill if it's near Brinkin – and then we could look for the twins!"

"We know most of the places near Swanage quite well and I don't remember a Brinkin village or Brinkin Hill at all," said Katie. "Let's get out the big map of Dorset and see if we can find it."

"Where is it?" asked Nick. "Oh, I know. It's in the cupboard with the guide books. I'll go and get it."

He found it, and the two of them spread out the big, detailed map on the floor and studied it carefully. Punch thought they were playing a game with him and kept walking all over it, sniffing at each place they touched. In the end, Nick pushed him out of the room and slammed the door. He barked miserably but as no one took any notice of him, he went off to the kitchen, hoping for a titbit.

Nick spotted Brinkin first and jabbed his finger on it triumphantly. "There you are! Brinkin. And look at these contour lines nearby, they're very close together, which shows a steep hill. I bet that's Brinkin Hill!"

"It's not terribly far from Swanage," said Katie, looking at the map. "We'd have to go through Corfe village, and take this little road here."

"Right. As soon as we get down to Swanage this year, let's hire two bikes and cycle to Brinkin Hill to find the twins!" cried Nick. "What a surprise we'll give them!"

CHAPTER 3

PUNCH HAS AN ACCIDENT

Nick and Katie lived next door to Mike and Penny. The boys were the same age, and Penny was a little younger than Katie. They got on well together although Penny was very inquisitive and always wanted to know what everyone was doing, which infuriated both Nick and her brother.

"Mike and Penny are back from Spain today," said Katie. "It's a pity that our holidays don't match this year – we go just after they come back but at least we'll see them before we go."

"Yes, isn't it? This time last year we were starting to plan that mystery that never was to amuse Uncle Bob," said Nick. "We had the most exciting two days of our lives."

Next day Nick and Katie, followed by Punch, ran down the garden and squeezed through the hole in the hedge. Nick whistled loudly as they walked towards

Mike's shed. Mike was there waiting and Punch ran up to him, his tail wagging wildly, nearly knocking him over in his excitement at seeing him again.

"Hi, Nick. Hi, Katie. Stop it, Punch! I've had a shower this morning already so I don't need a lick and polish now," he said, laughing and pushing Punch down. "Thanks for looking after my mice, Nick. They look wonderful and that last litter has really grown up now."

"Where's Penny, Mike?" asked Katie. "Is she indoors? We thought we might all go off for a walk, it's such a wonderful day."

"Smashing idea!" said Mike. "Go and find her, Katie."

Katie went up to the house, leaving Nick and Mike talking mice and Punch doing his best to lick them each in turn.

Penny was arranging her ornaments and pictures in her bedroom, which had been decorated while she'd been on holiday. She was very pleased to see Katie.

"I've just finished up here," she said. "If we go out, I can tell you all my news as we walk. I'll get some apples and biscuits to take with us and we'd better take some cans of drink as it's going to be really hot by midday."

Penny put things in a rucksack and they ran out to join the boys. Punch barked joyfully when he realised they were off for a walk and rushed ahead of them out of the gate.

"Let's go up Skylark Hill," suggested Nick. "I haven't got binoculars with me but there are plenty of birds to hear."

"I want to stop at the little shop before we turn off for the hill," said Mike. "I need some more film for my camera. I took a lot of photos when we were away."

Punch was in front of them, sniffing in the hedge, barking at birds, and nearly tripping the children up when he ran under their feet after a particularly interesting smell.

Then he disturbed a tabby cat that had been asleep under a bush. She darted out and streaked across the road. Without hesitating, Punch dashed after her and straight under the wheels of a car.

The car screeched to a stop as the children ran to where Punch lay, unmoving and bleeding from a great gash on his head.

Katie and Penny were in tears. Nick knelt down and stroked Punch gently but he didn't respond.

"Speak to him, Nick. Let him hear your voice," said Mike, bending down.

"Punch, can you hear me? Oh, Punch, please wag your tail just a tiny bit," said Nick, half crying. "He can't hear me, Katie, and he's bleeding so much."

Katie knelt beside him. "Cover him with my sweater so he doesn't get cold. It doesn't matter about the blood. Oh, poor old Punch."

At that moment, the driver of the car came up. "I'm so sorry. I never saw your dog as I came round the bend. He ran straight at me and I had no time to avoid him."

"He was after a cat," said Mike. "He's in a bad way. We ought to take him to the vet at once but I'm not sure if the surgery is open still."

"It's open for another half-hour and I know where it is. Let me take him there in the car. He ought to be seen as quickly as possible."

Nick nodded. The man lifted Punch up

very gently and laid him on the back seat.

"May my sister and I come with him?" asked Nick.

"Yes. Sit one each side of him and steady him," the man said. "I'm Bob Jordan, by the way."

"We'll follow you," Penny said, as Mr Jordan got into the car and drove off.

When Mike and Penny reached the surgery, they found Nick and Katie sitting inside, waiting. Mr Jordan had gone to report the accident to the police.

"The vet's examining Punch now," said Katie. "She saw him straight away as soon as Mr Jordan brought him in."

"Is he still unconscious?" asked Penny hesitantly.

"Yes," replied Nick. "I'm really afraid he's going to die. Oh, I couldn't bear to be without him."

"Nor could I," said Katie, crying again. "I can't believe I might never hear him bark again, or feel him lick me." Nick bit his lip to keep himself from crying.

"Did the vet say how long she'd be?" asked Mike. "Would you like Penny and me to run home and get your mother?"

"No, she's out this afternoon," answered Katie. At that moment the vet came out.

"Punch will be all right, I think," she said. "I'm going to keep him here until tomorrow morning because he has concussion and I want to watch him. I've stitched up the nasty cut on his head and he's stopped bleeding. He's torn the muscles in his left front leg and he's bruised and scratched but there doesn't seem anything else wrong. He's a lucky little dog!"

"Please may we see him before we go?" asked Katie and Nick.

The vet said they could slip in and give him a pat before he went downstairs to a recovery kennel. Punch lay quite still but the blood had been cleaned away and he was breathing quietly. Nick and Katie stroked him gently. "Please get better, Punch," whispered Nick.

That evening, the vet telephoned Nick and Katie's mother. The children stood by her, trying to listen.

"What did she say, Mum? How is Punch?" the children asked, when she'd put the receiver down.

"She says that Punch is conscious again and seems better. If all is well in the morning he can come home," said Mrs Terry. "But he needs rest for a few days and his leg is quite badly damaged. I don't think he'll be able to come on holiday with us, I'm afraid."

"I'm so pleased he's going to get better," said Katie. "But we'll really miss him on holiday."

"I don't care about the holiday as long as Punch is all right," said Nick. "I'll stay here and look after him myself. I could always sleep at Mike's."

"Then I'll stay with you," said Katie firmly.

"No," said Mrs Terry. "Of course you can't stay here on your own."

"I think we might be able to arrange for Mike and Penny to look after Punch at their house," said Mr Terry. "You've looked after Mike's mice for him several times now. There are still five days before you go away, and he won't need much looking after by then, except visiting the vet to see that the leg is healing properly."

"That's a very good idea," said Mrs

Terry. "I'll go and telephone Mike's mother now."

She was smiling when she came back. "That's all arranged. Mike and Penny would love to look after him and Mike's mother will take him to the vet for his appointments."

A few minutes later, a delighted Mike and Penny arrived.

"Oh, I'm so glad that Punch is going to get better," said Penny happily. "I'll brush him every day while he's with us."

"And I shall really enjoy having a dog around the place," said Mike. "By the time you come back, Punch will be walking for miles."

"In the autumn, I'm going to take Punch to dog-training classes and teach him never to run out into the road again, even if there is a cat around," said Nick. "I don't ever want to see my dog lying bleeding and unconscious in the road again."

"Punch loves you both a lot," said Katie. "Thanks for saying you'll have him – he'll be much happier with you than going to kennels."

CHAPTER 4

SETTLING IN

The night before their holiday, the children packed up Punch's bowls, brush, lead, blanket and enough food to last him three weeks. Then they went down the garden, squeezed through the hole in the hedge and walked up to Mike's shed. Nick gave a piercing whistle and Mike came out to meet them. Punch tried to jump up but he couldn't manage it with his leg in plaster, so he wagged his tail and licked Mike's shoes. Mike rubbed his ears and patted him.

"Let me help with all these tins of food. Hey, he's going to eat a lot, isn't he!" he exclaimed, taking some of the bags from Katie.

Penny piled things neatly under the mouse cage where she had cleared a space. "What did the vet say about Punch's leg today?" she asked. "Has he still got to keep the plaster on?"

"Yes, and he doesn't like it a bit. He'll have to wear a plastic collar round his head if he goes on trying to bite it off," Nick answered. "He's doing very well, the vet says, but he's got to keep it on for another week and then she'll look at it again. Here's his appointment card."

"Mum said we've got to get straight back, because we haven't finished packing yet," said Katie. "Is it all right if we bring Punch over here about eight o'clock tomorrow? We'll be having an early breakfast because Mum wants to call in on Granny and her friend about mid-morning with some things she needs."

"Okay. See you at eight," said Mike. "I'm usually here feeding the mice by then."

They said goodnight and Nick and Katie ran off home with Punch, who was a little puzzled to see all his things left with Mike and Penny.

The next day the children woke up early. The sun was shining in a clear blue sky and it looked like being a very hot day. After breakfast they took Punch round to Mike and Penny. Mike was in his shed but Penny hadn't got out of bed yet.

"I hate saying goodbye to Punch," said Katie. "He does love coming on holiday with us. He adores paddling and chasing all the little waves down the beach."

"He also tries to grab any beach ball he can see and then runs off with it," said Nick. "He got into trouble several times last year."

"We'll take great care of him for you," said Mike. "Just as soon as he can walk properly again, I'll take him off for plenty of good walks."

At that moment Penny ran in. "I'm going to feed him and give him lots of cuddles," she said. "I don't think we'll want to give him back to you at the end of your holiday!"

Katie and Nick fussed over Punch. "Be a good dog and do what Mike and Penny tell you. I'm very sorry you can't come with us," said Nick, scratching his ears.

Katie hugged him. "I'm going to miss you so much but I'll send you a delicious postcard smeared with fish!" she said.

"You'll be very popular with the postman!" said Nick with a grin. "Bye, Punch – don't forget us!"

A horn tooted next door. "Right, we must go and help pack the car. Come on, Katie," said Nick.

With a last pat for Punch they rushed out of the shed, shutting the door so Punch wouldn't follow them. He tried to, of course. He barked and barked and nearly scratched a hole in the door. He didn't want to be left behind at all.

Back at home, Nick and Katie found the car nearly packed.

"Hurry up," called their mother. "Go and get the boxes of food from the hall and all the loose things like tennis rackets."

The family were renting the same house that they had stayed in for several years. They took games and books for rainy days, camping gear and picnic things for fine weather, so with clothes, tennis rackets and Mrs Terry's golf bag the car was very full.

Mr Terry had helped them pack the car but he wasn't coming with them. He had to go to New York on a business trip but hoped to join them later.

"Be good and look after your mother," he said. "I wish I were coming with you, but I promise I'll be back in time to be with you for the third week of the holiday."

They waved goodbye and set off on their journey. "I wish Dad could come the whole time," said Katie. "I love swimming and playing tennis and walking with him."

"So do I," agreed Nick. "He's always worrying about work at home, but when he's away he's quite different, he relaxes."

"I wish he could come too; he needs a rest," said Mrs Terry. "But he's positive that there's nothing to stop him joining us after his New York trip."

Gran welcomed them to her friend's house and gave them drinks and a snack. She was very pleased to see them but sorry to hear about Punch. She said she was enjoying exploring old churches and looking round National Trust gardens with her friend.

They had lunch at a village pub, sitting outside under a shady tree. "We've made very good time," said Mrs Terry. "I'm going to drive the rest of the way on little country roads and we should arrive about four o'clock with plenty of time to unpack and have a walk before supper."

At last they came to Corfe village with its

ruined castle standing high on a grassy mound in the centre.

"We must go to the castle again," said Nick. "I love the cottages huddled round the mound. They were mostly built with stone from the castle after Cromwell's troops destroyed it."

"Nearly there now," his mother said as they left Corfe village. "I'll be quite glad to take my eyes off the road and just look at blue sea."

Their house was waiting for them, clean

and welcoming. The car was soon emptied and the cases unpacked. The holiday had really begun!

"Three whole weeks!" said Nick in delight. "We'll swim and ride and sail and, of course, we'll go to Brinkin Hill. If only it's the same place that the twins meant in their letter!"

Swanage was just the same as ever, a great wide bay of forget-me-not blue, with hardly a ripple or a wave except where it lapped the sand. Behind rose the glorious hills. The sun shone warmly, and the very first thing that Nick and Katie did was to fling off their clothes, put on swimming things and prance into the water.

"Ooooh – it's cold after all," said Katie in surprise. "And it looked so warm!"

"Tomorrow is the very first day of the very first week," said Nick, splashing Katie, "and the first days will go beautifully slowly. Then they'll glide away at top speed without being noticed. But oh, how fantastic the very beginning is."

"Yes – with heaps of time in front of you," said Katie, who was in the water properly now and swimming beside Nick.

"Oh, this patch of water is lovely and warm. I'm going to turn over and float in it."

The next day the two children wandered down into the town. They went to the sailing club to find Mr Willard who had taken them sailing the last two years. He had a five-metre dinghy that he took them out in and was teaching them how to handle.

"I do hope he's here today," said Katie, looking all round. "You can't miss him. With his black hair and beard and his ruggedness, he'd look just like a pirate if he tied a red scarf round his head."

"He's a marvellous teacher. He never loses patience even when you do silly things like gybing by mistake," said Nick thoughtfully. "I envy the children at his school, I bet he makes everything really interesting."

They found Mr Willard and arranged to go out in the dinghy the next day. He hadn't changed a bit and seemed pleased to see them again.

"How about a bit of mackerel fishing this evening?" he asked. "Plenty of them around, and pollock too."

"Yes, that would be great," said Nick.

"We'll catch some for supper. We can grill them ourselves to save Mum cooking!"

That evening they all went out in a rowing-boat with the fishing-lines. Both Nick and Katie could row well, though Katie found it quite tough if the sea was choppy. They fixed bits of bicycle valve on the fish hooks and cast the lines overboard. The fish nibbled at first and then they took the bait. After an hour the three of them had caught a dozen mackerel and a number of pollock.

"Well, that should do us for supper tonight," said Mr Willard. "My wife's waiting for them at home, so we'll row back to shore now."

"I like mackerel best, but pollock are good if you cook them as soon as they've been caught," Nick said.

"That was fun," Katie told her mother later on, as they ate the freshly grilled fish. "It's almost my favourite meal I think, especially when I've caught them."

Another day Mrs Terry drove them to Studland Heath to bird-watch. They took a picnic lunch with them and after lunch Mrs Terry went up to the golf course, leaving the children on the heath. Mike had lent Nick his binoculars for the holiday but he promised to share them with Katie.

"I don't really mind, Nick," Katie said. "I'm going to look for wild flowers for my collection. The countryside here is different from where we live so I'll look for flowers I haven't found yet to press for the school flower competition."

The children walked towards Shell Beach and Katie found several new flowers. Nick took photographs of Poole Harbour and of some of the seabirds he saw. Then they walked back to Studland and met their mother for tea in a big hotel that had an adventure playground.

"That was a lovely afternoon," said Katie happily. "I wish Dad was with us though."

"He wouldn't have been with us," answered Nick. "He'd have been playing golf with Mum!"

"Ah, but when we got home, he'd be going swimming with you both," said their mother. "It's less than a fortnight before he's back with us and it'll go all too fast!"

CHAPTER 5

OFF TO FIND BRINKIN HILL

For the first few days Katie and Nick hardly thought of the twins at all. There were so many lovely things to do. Then Katie spoke about them.

"We've forgotten Sophie and David. What about cycling over to Brinkin to see if we can find the hill, and any house there that the twins might be living in? I'd love to see them again and it's a shame to waste time when they might only be staying for a fortnight."

"Okay, let's go over today," said Nick. "We'll ask Mum to give us some sandwiches. We'd better go down to the cycle shop and hire a couple of bikes."

The two children went into Swanage and managed to hire two bicycles. "If Brinkin Hill is as steep as it looks on the map, we won't be sorry we spent extra on these extra gears," said Nick.

At ten thirty they were ready to set off on their bikes, each carrying a backpack containing bags of food and a couple of other items. Nick had brought the binoculars with him too and Katie had packed the new camera she'd been given for her birthday.

"You can buy yourselves drinks," their mother said. "And I have no doubt you will fill yourselves up with ice creams, too. I'll expect you back when I see you. Take care and have a good day!"

The two cycled off. They took the Corfe Castle direction and marvelled, as always, when they came to the ancient little village, dominated by the centuries-old ruined castle, dreaming by itself high upon the hill.

"There's such a lovely old feeling here," said Katie as they cycled round the hill on which the castle stood. The jackdaws wheeled above it, calling *chack-chack-chack* in their loud, cheerful voices. "Phew, isn't it hot, Nick? I could do with an ice cream and a drink already; couldn't you?"

"Let's get just a bit thirstier and hotter, then we'll enjoy them all the more," said

Nick. So on they went, panting in the hot sun though they only wore shorts and tee-shirts.

They turned off the main road to a lane signposted to Brinkin. It was a big village lying in a little hollow surrounded by trees, with a farm or two spread out on either side. Behind rose a very steep hill, closely wooded.

"I should think that must be Brinkin Hill," said Nick. "But why have the twins come here? There don't seem to be many houses, and it's a long way to the sea if they want to sail and fish like they did last year."

"It does seem strange," admitted Katie. "But how will we go about finding them? Just knock on every door and ask if they've seen a pair of red-haired twins?"

"Let's find a shop that sells ice creams and ask if the hill is called Brinkin Hill," answered Nick practically. "There'll only be a couple of shops in the village and the twins are sure to buy ice creams in one of them. So they should be easy to find."

They soon found a shop. It was a typical village shop, half post office and half everything else. It seemed to sell potatoes as well as stamps, drinks, crisps and ice cream, as well as postal orders, sunhats, socks, rope, kettles, saucepans, chocolate and much else besides.

"This is the kind of shop I like," said Nick, looking round. "If I had a shop I would have one just like this."

"Yes, and keep it all muddly, too," said Katie. "I can just see your shop, Nick – you'd never be able to find a thing!"

They sat on a little seat outside, drank out of the cans and licked the ice cream out of the cornets.

"Delicious!" said Katie. "I hope the person who invented ice cream had medals hung all over him!"

They took the empty cans back and spoke to the old lady behind the post office counter.

"Could you tell us if that is Brinkin Hill over there?"

"You're right," said the old woman in her pleasant country voice. "That be Brinkin Hill, but don't you be going there. It's too steep."

"Does anyone live up on the hill?" asked Katie.

"Well, there's an old house there, Brinkin Towers," said the woman. "Been shut up for years, it has, yes – and no one durst go near it, for 'tis said there were strange goings-on there once. One day my old ma went up there for a prank when she were a girl, and she heard weeping and wailing fit to break your heart. So she said."

"Does anyone live there now?" repeated Nick.

"Not a soul has taken that path up the hill for years far as I know," said the old woman. "I tell you, don't you go near the place – it's bad. There's a high wall round it too and you can hardly see the old house, except for its towers showing above the trees."

"What about the other side of the hill? Does the road go down there or does it end at Brinkin Towers?" asked Katie.

"No," answered the old woman. "Road be a dead end. Walkers come down here sometimes from t'other side, but 'tis a hard climb both ways."

The children thanked her and went off, disappointed.

"Sounds as if it's most unlikely the twins

would be there," said Nick. "What shall we do?"

"Remember that note Sophie flung out of the car, hoping it would reach us?" said Katie. "She sounded really worried and it's very strange that no one told them where they were going. Even stranger that they weren't able to post a letter to us. I think we ought to look at any house that they could possibly have been taken to."

"I still think the twins were making up a mystery with all those dire hints in their letter," said Nick. "I think we should turn back and perhaps go further along the main road and take the next turning. It might go to the other side of Brinkin Hill and we could look for houses there."

"Last year, you and Mike made up a mystery that turned out to be true, so maybe theirs is too," said Katie. "I think we should go on up the hill. I want to see what Brinkin Towers is like. Come on – there's no harm in trying."

CHAPTER 6

UP TO BRINKIN TOWERS

The children got on their bicycles and rode off in the direction of the hill. They came to a steep road that led upwards. It was just a narrow lane, and as the hedges had not been clipped for years, hawthorn and other trees were almost touching overhead.

Nick jumped off his bicycle and so did Katie. It was impossible to ride up such a steep lane. It was a very stony road, too, and they didn't want to get punctures from the flints that lay about.

It was very quiet, the silence only broken by the occasional call of a bird or the bark of a distant dog. The sun was hot but the high hedges and trees shaded the two children from the worst of the heat. The lane grew narrower as it went up, and soon became overgrown with weeds and grass, making walking a little easier.

"No car could possibly come up here

with the lane in this condition, Katie," said Nick. "And see here? There's bramble right across the road, from one side of the hedge to the other. It really does look as if nobody's been this way for years. Let's go back."

"All right – go back then," said Katie, feeling hot and cross as she struggled uphill pushing her bike, but still determined to continue. "I'm going on by myself. It's just like you to give up."

"It is not," said Nick, setting off at once. "If you're going on, then so am I. Though there doesn't seem any point."

They went on in silence, except for puffs and pants. Little streams of perspiration ran down their faces, and their clothes stuck to their bodies. They began to long for another ice cream and a drink. No, two ice creams and two drinks! Perhaps even three.

The lane curved suddenly, and then came to a complete stop outside a great wooden gate that was crossed and re-crossed with iron bars in a strange pattern. The two children stood in front of it, staring up. It was very high and the top was set with wicked-looking iron spikes.

"Wow, look at that! It might be the gate of some castle," said Nick. He went up to it and pushed it. It did not move in the least, of course, but stood there, solid and immovable.

"Bolted from inside, I suppose," he said. "Look, there's a piece of ivy that has grown from the wall half across the gate!"

"Yes, and that definitely proves that no one has been through this gate for ages," said Katie, at once, "or the ivy would have been wrenched off when the gate was opened. No one can possibly live here now, that's obvious."

"What an incredibly high wall goes all round it," said Nick. "And set with those awful spikes too. They really meant to keep people out. If there were strange goings-on here, as that old woman hinted, the owners didn't want anyone to know about them!"

"The lane ends here so we can't go to the top of Brinkin Hill. Why don't we walk round the wall and see how far that goes?" said Katie, putting her bicycle against a tree. "We'll go all the way round the grounds and back again to this gate. That's if we can make our way all right."

"You do think of mad ideas," groaned Nick, but as he couldn't bear Katie to do anything without him, he put his bicycle down too, and followed her.

It was very difficult in places to make their way round the wall. Bushes and trees grew right up to it, and the undergrowth was so thick that the two children had to force their way through it.

"I think this is stupid," said Nick again. "We need to hack our way through some of this undergrowth if we're going to find the gate again. Let's turn back."

"No, that's silly. We must be more than halfway round already!" said Katie. "It will be quicker to get to the gate if we go on."

Nick followed Katie. For a while they struggled forwards, scratched by brambles and slashed by low branches, then Katie stopped with a sudden exclamation. They had come out on to a clear piece of hillside. They looked down a grassy slope, not at Brinkin village, which was now on the other side of the hill, of course, but on a curious little lake, set thickly round with trees. The still water shone blue as the sky. Not far from the shore of the secret lake was a small island full of trees. In the midst of the trees was a strange building with delicate rounded towers.

"Look at that!" said Katie, suddenly speaking in a whisper, though she couldn't think why. "A lake! It wasn't marked on the map, was it?"

"Too small, perhaps," said Nick. "And too secret! Why, nobody except the people who lived here would be able to see that lake, I should think. I wonder what that funny little building is on the island, it looks very odd, somehow, as if it didn't quite belong there!"

"I expect it's a summerhouse. It's too far from the lakeside to be a boathouse," said Katie. "What a fantastic view! I wonder how the people got down to the lake from Brinkin Towers, Nick. The lake must have belonged to the house. How on earth did they reach it?"

"There must be a way down," said Nick. Then he looked at Katie, suddenly struck by a bright idea. "And what's more there must be a door set in this side of the wall, so that the people who lived here could walk down from the grounds to the lake.

They wouldn't go out of that big front gate and walk all the way round the walls, as we have."

"Let's look for a door in the wall then, shall we?" said Katie, excited. "It can't be far from here."

They walked on round the thick, high wall for some way, and then Katie gave a sudden shout. "Nick! Here it is. A little door set deep in the wall. Look!"

Sure enough there was a door, and leading up to it was a path from the lake. The children stared at it in silence. Then Nick spoke.

"Several people have been here lately. It's all trampled, look. Someone's been in through this door, and nobody knows about them. Who are they, Katie? That's what I'd like to know!"

CHAPTER 7

INSIDE THE WALLS

Katie went to the door in the thick wall and pushed at it. She turned the looped iron handle, but the door wouldn't open.

"Locked on the other side, Katie," said Nick, in a low voice. "Whoever came here has entered secretly, and you can be sure every door will be locked and bolted. But isn't it weird?"

"Yes. Why should several people come from the lake and get into the house this way instead of up the lane to the front gate?" said Katie, puzzled. "Nick, you don't think the twins could possibly be here, do you?"

"I shouldn't think so," said Nick. "I can't see why anyone would come for a holiday to this peculiar place. It's so out of the way. I dare say there's some explanation for the trampled path. Perhaps someone comes in each day to look after the house."

"Where from?" demanded Katie at once. "If it were anyone from the village it would be known, and there doesn't seem to be a single cottage nearby."

"I suppose we can't possibly get into the grounds, can we?" said Nick, after a pause. "I think, if there's any chance of the twins being here, which, of course, I don't really believe, we ought to try and see them and find out what's happening. I know you've been worried because their last letter sounded so odd."

"Yes, I have. But how do you think we are going to climb over that very high wall, especially with those awful spikes on top?" said Katie scornfully. "I don't want to be jabbed to pieces, even if you do!"

An overgrown path cut with steps led down to the secret lake. The children didn't think they would follow it. Somehow they felt safer up by the wall.

"Let's carry on round the wall," said Nick at last. "It's about the only thing left to do."

So they went on again, pushing their way through the undergrowth, until suddenly Nick clutched at Katie and stopped her.

He pointed silently upwards.

She looked up to the top of the wall. A tree had fallen against it just there and had broken off the top layer of the bricks with their ugly spikes. There was a gap without spikes!

"We could shin up the tree and see over the wall from the top there, where it's broken," whispered Nick. "It's not a difficult climb because the tree slopes nicely."

Katie nodded. An excited feeling welled up in her, and she felt suddenly out of breath. She watched Nick climb carefully up the tree that leaned against the wall, and then sit on the top, where it was broken. Katie followed him, tearing her shorts on a sharp twig, but not even noticing it.

There wasn't room for both children at the top of the wall, as the gap was not very large. Katie peeped over Nick's shoulder.

They saw a great house with towers at each end. Little of the lower part of the building was visible because high trees surrounded it. They gazed at the big dark windows, but most of them had thick curtains pulled right across. It looked very

gloomy and quite uninhabited.

One window, up on the second floor, had its curtains drawn back and, as Nick and Katie watched, they saw a movement behind the window. Then a face looked out, but what kind of face they were too far away to see.

Katie clutched Nick and made him jump so much that he nearly fell off the wall.

"Don't," he whispered fiercely. "What's up? Did you see someone at the window too?"

"Yes. Who is it?" whispered Katie. "Oh, Nick, it might be the twins, and if they're locked up here, no one would ever know. They've got no parents or relations."

"It probably isn't the twins," said Nick gruffly. "But all the same, we'll try and find out. There's definitely something very odd about all this. People arriving secretly at this deserted old house; coming to that door in the wall instead of through the village, up the lane and in at the front gate. Who are they anyway, and why should they have brought the twins with them?"

"Can we grab hold of that tree branch growing against the inner side of the wall?"

said Katie. "It looks easy to climb down."

"Okay. But don't miss getting hold of the branch," said Nick. "I'll go first. And mind, if anyone meets us, we're only exploring. Don't say a word about the twins."

Soon they were both over the wall and down on the ground. The undergrowth was as thick here as on the other side of the wall, even thicker, it seemed to Katie, whose legs and hands were getting very scratched indeed. So were Nick's, but he didn't seem to notice.

They made their way cautiously towards the house, hiding behind trees whenever they trod on a twig that cracked, in case anyone had heard it. As they got closer, they wormed their way along the ground from bush to bush. But there seemed to be nobody about at all.

They stood at last behind a little summerhouse from where they could see the second-floor window that had no curtains drawn across it. They both peered up. No face was at the window now.

"What shall we do next?" whispered Nick. "I daren't go to find a door as we'd have to pass windows on the ground floor, and if they had the curtains drawn back, we might be seen."

"Couldn't we throw a stone up to that second-floor window?" said Katie. "If there's someone there, they will hear the noise of the stone and come to the window. Then we can see if it's the twins or not."

"Right, I'll try it," said Nick. He found two or three small stones and threw one up. It hit the wall just under the window. He tried again, and his aim was not only good, but much too hard!

Crash! The window broke. What a tremendous noise it seemed to make in those still grounds! Nick and Katie leaped back behind the summerhouse immediately. Now what would happen?

CHAPTER 8

A GREAT SURPRISE

Behind the summerhouse the two children began to tremble with excitement and sudden fear. Nick hadn't meant to break the window. What a dreadful thing to do! Ought he to go and own up?

Above them, from the second-floor room, there came the sound of a window being opened and thrown up. An angry voice was heard.

"You must have broken the window yourselves! Who else could do it? There's no one in the grounds at all!"

Nick, back in the shadow of the summerhouse again, stared upwards at the open window. A woman was leaning out, looking all around. Behind her pressed two other people. Nick's heart gave a sudden jump.

The other two were David and Sophie, the twins! There wasn't any doubt of it at all, because both were redheads – and it was two fiery heads that craned over the woman's shoulders. She pushed them back roughly.

"You'll be punished for this," she said in a sharp voice, and crashed the window down again. Katie and Nick didn't dare to stir; but as there was no further sound or movement, Nick whispered in Katie's ear:

"Let's stay here. The twins know they didn't break the window and as soon as that woman has gone out of the room, I bet they'll open the window and peer out to see who threw the stone. We'll just have to wait until they get the chance. Go right behind the summerhouse in case that woman comes outside to see if anyone's about."

So they waited patiently, and after about ten minutes they heard the squeak of the window being very cautiously opened. Nick peeped warily out from behind the summerhouse. Both twins were now hanging out of the window, trying to see out as far as possible.

Nick remembered the little whistling call that he and Katie had used the summer before when they had gone to fetch the twins out to play. He whistled the signal softly but clearly, sounding rather like a bird.

The twins above were transfixed with surprise. They almost fell out of the window trying to see into the garden below. Nick whistled again.

And back came David's answering whistle, just as it used to do the summer before:

"*Tui-tui-tui-too. Tuiti-too.*"

Then there was a whispered conversation between the twins and Sophie disappeared. David remained at the window, occasionally whistling softly, and answered cautiously by Nick below.

At last Sophie came back, looked out and then threw a ball of screwed-up paper. Luckily it fell near the summerhouse where Katie and Nick were hiding, too afraid to allow themselves to be seen. Nick reached out and picked up the ball of paper.

Sophie saw it disappear behind the summerhouse and whispered excitedly to David, who squinted down in great curiosity. Nick opened the screwed-up paper with trembling hands.

Sophie had scribbled a note to them,

her writing wobbling with hurry and excitement.

> *I say, is it really you? We knew your whistle at once. How did you find us? We're PRISONERS here! I'm sure of it.*
>
> *We were told by Miss Twisley (old Lawley's replacement) before we went that we were to be taken to somewhere very secret as our guardians were afraid we might be kidnapped because of our money – and the awful ruby! But we think we've been kidnapped anyway.*
>
> *Someone has double-crossed our guardians, and here we are, tucked away where nobody can find us – except you. Any idea how we can escape?*
>
> *Sophie*

Katie and Nick read the note together, amazed and shocked. They looked at one another.

"But what can we do?" whispered Katie. "Go home and tell Mum, I suppose – or the police."

"No," said Nick. "At least, we can tell Mum we've discovered that the twins are staying near Corfe, but we'd better not tell her anything else or get in touch with the police until we've talked to the twins. Look, Katie, if they really have been kidnapped, it's been done by bad and desperate men. They might . . . they might do something awful to the twins if they thought they'd been discovered. As soon as they saw people at the front gate demanding to be let in, they would have plenty of time to cover up all signs that Sophie and David had been here, and hide the ruby, too, if they've got it. Then the twins might never be heard of again."

This was a very long speech and Katie listened to it in silence. Then she thought about it.

"I think you're right," she said at last. "But if we don't tell Mum or the police, what else is there to do?"

"Could we possibly rescue them ourselves?" whispered Nick. "If we could get them out of the house somehow, they could easily climb over that gap in the wall, and come home with us. That would be the most sensible thing to do."

"What about the ruby?" asked Katie.

"Oh, who cares about that?" whispered Nick. "It's the twins we want. If you write a note, I'll wrap it round a stone and throw it up into the open window."

"I've got a pencil and some paper here," said Katie. "What shall I say?"

"Tell them we'll be back tomorrow. That woman may be suspicious today," said Nick. "Tell them to listen for our whistle."

Katie took out a little diary she always kept in her pocket and scribbled Nick's message on one of the pages. He found a stone and wrapped the page round it. It kept coming undone, so he took off his shoelace and tied the note firmly to the stone with it. Now to throw it!

He stood beside the summerhouse and took very careful aim. The stone flew straight up and in at the open window!

David and Sophie leaned out of the window and waved triumphantly to them. Then they quietly shut the window.

"Brilliant, Nick!" whispered Katie. "Now let's get away from here fast. I'll feel much happier when I'm on the other side of the wall!"

CHAPTER 9

Back Home – and a Clever Plan

Katie and Nick made their way cautiously through the tangled bushes and trees to the place where they had climbed over the wall. They clambered up the tree whose branch almost touched the wall, swung to the top where the spiked bricks had fallen away, and then shinned down the half-fallen tree the other side.

"I'm glad we're safely over," said Nick, still in a whisper. "Let's get back to our bikes."

"No. Let's sit down under a bush and have our lunch," said Katie. "We can see that beautiful little secret lake and the island in the middle of it from here. How I'd like to camp in a place like that!"

"Wouldn't it be safer to go back to our bikes?" said Nick. He had had quite enough of Brinkin Hill for one day.

"No. Oh, bother, yes! We'll have to fetch

our food, of course, and it's in the rucksacks where we left the bikes," said Katie. "You go and fetch it, Nick, and I'll find a nice place to sit."

Nick went off, grumbling to himself. It was Katie who wanted to picnic overlooking the lake, so why couldn't she go and fetch the food? Girls! He came back with the food and found Katie sitting in the shade of a large beech tree. She was gazing down at the little lake.

"I do like it," she said to Nick. "I'd love to go and explore down there. Could we?"

"No, we couldn't," said Nick shortly. "It's almost two o'clock already, no wonder we're starving! And I don't mind telling you that as soon as we've finished, we're biking down to get a drink at that village shop – a lovely, long, cool drink. I'm dying of thirst after walking to get the rucksacks."

Katie changed her mind about exploring when she thought of the long cool drink. The two sat together and ate fast, talking over the morning's happenings with their mouths full, there was such a lot to say.

When they had finished, they went on round the wall to their bicycles, gave a last glance at the great strong gate, and set off down the lane. They decided to walk, not to ride, because the hill was very steep, and there were so many flints and ruts halfway down. They were hot and thirstier than ever when they arrived at the village shop.

"You don't get many strangers here, I suppose," said Katie, to the old woman who had served them that morning.

"Oh no – we're right off the main road," said the old lady. "Why, I haven't seen a strange face, till yours today, not for four months, maybe!"

The children looked at one another, thinking the same thought. Whoever had gone to Brinkin Towers had gone another way then, a secret way! They obviously didn't want anyone to see them.

"Who owns Brinkin Towers now?" asked Nick.

"Oh, they say it belongs to a rich man who lives far away over the seas," said the old woman. "Anyways, seems he's forgotten all about it. One of these days it will fall into rack and ruin, the rain will get into the roof and owls and rats will live in it, nobody else. But don't you go there, now –

I've warned you. It's a strange place, and there were strange goings-on long ago. For all we know there's strange things still going on!"

Little did she know how right she was! The children almost chuckled. They threw their empty cans in the litter bin and went off again, feeling better.

They stopped at Corfe village and had an early tea much too soon after their late lunch. Afterwards they climbed the grassy mound to the ruined castle where only the tower was still standing. Jackdaws flew around it or settled on the broken window ledges as they called to each other with the metallic *chack*, *chack* that Nick and Katie remembered from previous visits. The little tree, growing through a paving stone, was slightly bigger and the grass was full of daisies. The children lay in a warm corner of the ruined courtyard and dozed in the sunshine.

"Oh, I'm hot," said Nick, with a yawn. "Let's go back home, get changed and go swimming. The tide should be fairly full now so we won't have so far to walk!"

"Good idea. By the time we've cycled

back, we'll have reached melting point, I should think," agreed Katie.

They rode home and put their things away. Their mother had left a note saying that she was playing golf, so they changed into swimming things and went down to the beach. Little waves were breaking high up the sand and both children ran straight into the water, shrieking. Nick was wearing a waterproof watch and he and Katie timed each other diving and swimming under water.

Sometime later they sauntered back to their house and found their mother hurrying about.

"Oh, there you are!" she called. "Did you have a nice day? I'm afraid I've got bad news – Dad's secretary has just telephoned from London to say that his Aunt Jill has hurt her leg and has asked if I would go and look after her for a few days. Poor old thing, she'll be in quite a state with her arthritis as well."

"Are you going, Mum?" asked Nick.

"I'm afraid I shall have to," replied Mrs Terry. "There's no one else to help her because of the holidays."

"What about us? We haven't got to go, too, have we?" asked Katie in alarm.

"Oh no. You can't miss your holiday," said her mother. "I thought you could manage for a few days without me. I've spoken to Mrs Hall next door, and she'll keep an eye on you while I'm away. You could take the tent and camp out in the garden, as it's so very hot. I've been shopping and bought plenty of food, and you can always go and buy fish and chips, or eat at the little cafe across the road. I'll leave you enough spending money."

The two children cheered up at once. How lucky they didn't have to leave the cool blue sea in this hot weather!

"Camp out! It would be brilliant!" said Nick. "Can we choose where to pitch the tent, Mum?"

"Yes," said his busy mother, quite unsuspectingly. "Take your sleeping-bags, though. If you go to that field next door where all the other children are camping out this week, there'll be a grown-up to look after you, and the other children would be company for you."

But Katie and Nick had a better idea. As

soon as they had a minute alone they whispered excitedly together.

"We'll go and camp on that secret lake, on the little island!" said Katie. "And I'm sure we'll be able to think of a good plan for rescuing Sophie and David if we've a few days to do it in."

"Right," said Nick, finding the secret lake suddenly very tempting. "Just think, Katie, we'll be able to slip into the water a hundred times a day – and I bet that lake will be as warm as toast!"

"Oh, what fun!" said Katie. "Poor Aunt Jill, I'm very sorry she's broken her leg, but if she had to do it, she couldn't have chosen a better time!"

"I agree," said Nick, and then went on: "Katie, I think we'll have to tell Mum that we're going to see the twins tomorrow. We can say that they're staying near Corfe and that we might camp by their little lake for a couple of days. We won't say that they've been kidnapped, though."

"That's a good idea," replied Katie thoughtfully. "We can't be certain we'll be able to rescue them tomorrow, and if it takes longer and Mum telephones Mrs Hall, she'll be worried about us."

"Okay then," said Nick. "We'll be bringing Sophie and David back here anyway, so let's go and tell Mum that when she comes back again she'll find four children here to welcome her instead of two!"

CHAPTER 10

Off on a Real Adventure

Early the next morning Nick helped their mother to put her things in the car, while Katie got breakfast ready. Mrs Terry was anxious to leave as soon as possible since it was a long drive to the north of England where Aunt Jill lived. Over breakfast she talked to the two children.

"I've seen Mrs Hall and told her you're going to visit the twins today and might spend a couple of nights with them. She's quite happy if you bring them home with you – she remembers them from last year. Let her know when you come back or else she'll think you're burglars!" she said, with a smile. "You can call Mrs Hall if you get into any difficulties. I'll telephone around nine o'clock tonight to let you know how Aunt Jill is. I've written down her phone number for you, as well as Dad's secretary's."

"I'll write them in my little diary," said Katie. "I always have it with me."

"What about spending money?" asked Nick.

"There's some locked in the little case in my bedroom cupboard that you can take with you today," replied their mother. "I've given extra to Mrs Hall and you'll probably need to ask her for it if David and Sophie come back with you."

They went out to the car together. The children's mother kissed them both goodbye, sorry to have to leave, but pleased that the weather looked set fine for camping.

"Goodbye, both of you, and don't get up to any mischief," she said. "Give Sophie and David my love and tell them I'm looking forward to seeing them again."

She waved goodbye to the two children and started up the car. They both waved back as she drove away down the road.

"Whatever would Mum have said if she knew we were off to rescue the twins?" said Nick, with a grin. "Come on, Katie! Let's go and get our kit packed."

Back indoors they spread their things out on the hall floor.

"Tent – sleeping-bags – food – swimming things – towels," recited Katie. "Toothbrushes – soap – hairbrush – comb – come on, you think of something too, Nick."

It didn't take very long to get ready. The two of them fixed boxes to the backs of their bicycles and piled everything into them, as well as into their rucksacks. By the time they had finished, their bicycles seemed twice as heavy as usual to pedal along.

They said goodbye to Mrs Hall and explained where they would be camping. She was delighted that David and Sophie would be coming back with them in a day or two.

"They really kept me on my toes when they stayed here last year," she said. "Crept into the kitchen to cut big slices of cake to take up to bed and thought I never noticed! Telephone me whichever day you decide to come back, and I'll bake their favourite chocolate cake!"

The two children picked up their loaded bikes, waved, and set off.

"Have you packed the tin-opener?" yelled Nick as they got under way. "There, I knew you wouldn't think of an important thing like that. You go and pack crowds of tins and never even think of bringing something to open them with."

"I can't think of everything," said Katie. "You can just turn back and get it yourself!"

They were ready to start off at last. Away they went, more slowly than the day before because of their heavy load. What fun to be heading straight into an adventure like this. And nobody knew!

They cycled through Corfe village and took the turning to Brinkin village. They stopped at the little shop to collect plenty of cans of lemonade and cola.

"My, you're going to have a fine time!" said the old lady, seeing all their gear. "Where are you going to camp?"

"Oh, somewhere near water so that we can swim," answered Nick at once, before Katie could say too much. "See you again sometime!"

They went off quickly and soon came to the steep Brinkin Hill. They wondered if there was a better way to the secret lake, but decided that there wasn't, or there would have been a signpost to it, it was such a beautiful spot. They decided to stick to the way they knew.

So, panting, they laboured up the hill till they came to the fast-shut gates. Then they painfully wheeled their bicycles through the undergrowth as they skirted the wall. At last they came to where the path led down to the lake. They debated what to do. Should they climb over the wall and try and speak to the twins, or find a camping place on the island?

"Let's hope there'll be a boat there," said Nick, "or I can see us swimming to the island with bundles tied to the tops of our heads, like people do in India!"

"There has to be some way of getting across," said Katie. "People must once have gone over to the building we saw there."

Nick decided to go over the wall and see if the twins answered to his whistle. He was soon hiding in a bush under the broken window. He whistled softly, and then, feeling braver, a little more loudly. There was no answer at all.

The window was shut, though still broken, and there was no face looking out. The twins must be somewhere else.

Well, it was no use waiting. He might as well go back to Katie and help her down to the little secret island with their luggage. Perhaps it would be a good idea to come back at night when there would be no danger at all of being seen.

Katie was delighted to see him, but disappointed to hear that he hadn't spoken to the twins. She agreed that the best thing would be to get down to the island and find a camping place, and to go back to Brinkin Towers when it was dark. There would be a moon to help them then.

They made their way down the steep hill to the little lake. They were weighed down with all their things and had to go very slowly indeed, because although there were steps cut out of the rocky hillside, they were overgrown, and worn by the weather. It was difficult to balance all their things and watch the steps at the same time.

At last they were down by the lakeside. The water was smooth, clear and very blue. The little island lay some way off, looking most inviting. The children could just see the domed towers of the strange building behind the trees that grew there.

"This looks like a boathouse," said Nick, going towards a broken-down, weather-beaten shed, built out halfway over the water on stilts. The door at the back was broken, and Nick stepped inside.

"There *is* a boat!" he said. "And it must still be all right, because it's floating. What mouldy old cushions inside. They smell disgusting!"

They found a couple of paddles hanging up. There were no oars to be seen, but as the boat was a very small one, that didn't matter.

"Spread out a sleeping-bag in the boat and we'll put all our things on that," said Katie. That was soon done. Then the two stepped gingerly into the boat and took a paddle each.

"It can't possibly matter using this old boat," said Nick, as he undid a half-rotten rope from a post. "Anyway, for all we know, it belongs to David and Sophie for the time being, if Brinkin Towers has been rented for them. Here goes!"

They paddled the boat out of its shed and into the hot sunshine. Lovely! Over the calm blue water went the two children, their boat moving quite fast.

"Look out, we're coming into shore," said Nick. "Island ahead, with a perfect little cove to pull into. Might be made for us!"

"Well, here we are," said Katie, gazing at the little island. "It's the very first time I've ever spent a night on an island. I hope we'll enjoy it!"

CHAPTER 11

ON THE LITTLE ISLAND

The two children pulled the boat up on to the sandy shore of the cove and then landed their belongings.

"Let's go and find a good place to camp," said Nick. "I wonder if anyone ever comes here. It doesn't look like it!"

They wandered over the island. It was very overgrown, but at one time it must have been laid out partly as a garden, for the children could still see roses flowering high in brambly bushes.

Then, suddenly, they came upon the strange building they had seen from the top of the hill. It was set in a grove of foreign-looking trees covered in pink blossom that had been planted in a square around it.

Inside the square stood the long, low building. Nick thought it looked like a temple. At each corner were graceful towers pointed at the top. Nick said they looked like minarets, but he wasn't sure. They didn't look like English church spires, anyway. In the centre was the dome, which was drawn into a slim pinnacle at its apex.

The windows were delicately arched, and the steps that led up to the intricately carved door were set with curious bits of coloured glass, dirty now, but gleaming here and there where one or two had been cleaned by heavy rain.

The children stood still listening warily to the silence that lapped the building. Even the birds seemed to have stopped singing. But there was nobody else in the temple grove. They went quietly up the steps and pushed at the beautiful door, but it was locked. They went to look in at the windows.

"Why, it's a kind of museum inside," said Katie in a whisper. "What are all those weird figures, Nick?"

"Idols, I should think," said Nick. "Statues of Indian gods. Look how they're sitting cross-legged, staring into space."

A nasty thought suddenly struck Katie. Indian gods! Wasn't it from India that the strange ruby had come? And hadn't the old woman in the shop said that she thought Brinkin Towers once belonged to a rich man from overseas? Suppose, just suppose, he was Indian and this place was his!

"And just suppose," said Katie, speaking out loud, "just suppose that the Indians want to get their sacred stone back again! If they kidnapped the owners, who are now Sophie and David, mightn't they bring them here to Brinkin Towers? Wow! I think I'm beginning to understand things now."

"What on earth are you talking about?" said Nick in astonishment.

Katie told him. "It all fits in, you see," she said when she had finished. "I don't know how they managed to take Sophie and David away like this, but it's the ruby they want, there's no doubt about that. I expect it once belonged to a statue rather like these."

They peered in at the window again. Katie shivered. The smiling figures sat there so still, their strange faces motionless, their jewelled eyes unwinking.

They tiptoed round all the windows, peering into the rooms. It certainly did seem like a museum, for not only were there carved figures but also great vases, wonderful jewelled swords, beautiful little statues, and hangings that had once been rich and magnificent.

"Nick, this window has come loose," said Katie, startled, as the window her face was pressed against suddenly swung inwards. "Anyone could get in here – look! It's surprising no thieves have been inside."

"For one thing, who would know there was such a place here?" said Nick. "All hidden away and secret, and, for another, I should think most people would be scared stiff by those figures. I feel pretty terrified myself."

Katie pulled at the window and tried to close it, but the hasp was broken. She caught sight of a statue just inside, staring at her with bright emerald eyes, and she scowled at him.

"Don't you glare at me like that," she said fiercely.

But, as he seemed to scowl back, she hurriedly went away to join Nick. Carved statues that scowled were definitely not suited to a brilliant August day.

They found a sheltered place to camp, in

a little glade. Through the trees they could see the blue water of the lake. Sunshine dappled the ground, and when the wind blew gently the dapples danced. It was really lovely.

"We won't go up to Brinkin Towers till it's dark," said Nick, taking off his clothes to swim. "Where are my swimming trunks? Oh, here they are. Coming, Katie?"

"I'm just going to arrange things a bit," said Katie. "Where shall we put up the tent, Nick? Or do you think we need to? Couldn't we just sleep outside in our sleeping-bags tonight? It's so incredibly hot."

"Yes, let's not bother about the tent," said Nick. "Let's just have the sky for a ceiling, and grass for a bed."

"What fun to bring Sophie and David back here," said Katie happily as she shook out the sleeping-bags.

"Better than that gloomy house," said Nick. "Now I'm going into the lake! Come when you're ready." And away he went through the trees, a lithe brown figure, and flung himself into the lake with a tremendous splash.

Katie soon followed, and the two swam lazily round the island. The lake water was cool and deep a little way from the island, but wonderfully clear. Near to the island the bed of the lake was soft and sandy so that the water was warmed by the sun.

"Let's go and lie in the sunshine and get dry," said Nick. "Then we'll eat a most enormous lunch. You know, I'm very sorry for grown-ups, Katie, it must be horrid not to feel hungry all the time, like we do!"

"I can't imagine ever not wanting huge meals or planning adventures," said Katie. "Yet even teenagers who have just left school, with time to go exploring and adventuring, don't want to. They prefer to go shopping or watch TV or dance all night."

"I know," said Nick. "And adults have to go out to work and bring up families and they forget about the fun of being young and all the exciting things there are to do."

The children had a wonderful day wandering round the island, bird-watching, swimming again and racing each other across the lake. They ate a large supper while they watched the sun sink down in a sky washed with rose-pink and orange.

The sun had quite gone now, though it was still warm. The only sounds disturbing the silence were the occasional call of an owl and the plop of a fish jumping in the lake.

"What time shall we go up to the house?" asked Katie at about ten o'clock, waking from a doze. "I shall fall fast asleep in a minute or two. Hadn't we better go soon? It's almost dark."

"There's the moon coming up," said Nick. "We may as well set off now. Here's good luck to us, Katie – and whatever you do, keep quiet!"

CHAPTER 12

INSIDE BRINKIN TOWERS

Katie and Nick went to the little cove, which was streaked with moonlight, and Katie stepped into the boat. Nick pushed off, and then leaped in himself. The children paddled in silence across to the mainland. It was a beautiful night, almost as light as day.

They tied the boat up quietly, and then made their way up the steep path to Brinkin Towers. Once at the top they walked carefully round the wall till they came to where they could climb over.

Up the tree, on to the broken wall-top, down the branch on the other side, and there they were, standing in the grounds once more. An owl hooted and made them both jump almost out of their skins.

"Come on! I think I can see a light in that second-floor room, where the twins were yesterday," whispered Nick. Keeping in the shadows, they made their way over to the great house and looked up.

The curtains were drawn over the open window, but through the crack shone a light. Were the twins there alone? The two children did hope so!

"I'm going to whistle very softly," said Nick. "I daren't do it loudly in case anyone is with the twins. But they both have very sharp ears, so if I whistle almost under my breath they'll hear me!"

He waited, listening for a moment. Then he whistled softly. *"Tui-tui-tui-too. Tuiti-too."* Holding their breath, the two waited in silence. Nothing happened for a moment or two, then the curtains were cautiously drawn a little way apart, and a head peeped out.

A very soft whistle came in answer. Then something dropped down from the window, just clipping Nick's ear as it passed. The curtains were pulled close again, so that the light showed through just a tiny crack, as before.

On the ground beside Nick lay a key, with a small label attached to it. He picked it up, surprised.

"There's a message on the label," whispered Nick, and he and Katie screwed up their eyes and tried to read it by moonlight.

The message was in Sophie's writing:

Key of garden door, round other side of the house. We got it by a trick today. Can you come in, creep up to our room and unlock our door? We know the key of our room is in the lock on the outside.

Hope you don't get caught! We'll push a piece of paper just under our door, so that you'll see it sticking out and know it's our room.

Sophie

The two stared at one another, delighted and half scared. They could get into the house if the garden door was only locked and not bolted. They could make their way upstairs, and unlock the twins' door, and then escape would be easy!

"Come along, let's find the garden door," whispered Katie. They went cautiously round the house, glad that where once gravel paths had been there were now only weeds and grass. Their footsteps could not possibly be heard.

On the other side of the house was a little side door. "This must be the one," whispered Nick, and he slid the key into the lock. It turned easily – fortunately, without even a squeak. Now, was it bolted as well as locked? He pushed hard and the door opened. What a bit of luck!

They crept into a dark passage. Nick paused and Katie bumped into him.

"I'm just trying to get my bearings," he whispered. "Let me see, the twins' room is on the other side of the house. Let's find the stairs and go up."

"There may be back stairs," whispered Katie. "It would be safer to go up those than the main stairs."

"Good idea," said Nick. He crept forward cautiously, and came into a dimly-lit hall, a great place full of enormous pieces of old furniture and heavy hangings. Black shadows lurked in the far corners, and Nick couldn't help wondering if anyone was hiding there, waiting for him. His knees began to feel a bit shaky.

Rooms opened off the hall. One room

had its door slightly ajar, and a beam of light streamed out. That was clearly a room to be avoided. Where was the kitchen? If there was no one there, they might find the back stairs and creep up.

They saw a green baize door in a far corner. "That must be the way to the kitchen," whispered Nick in Katie's ear. "Come on, as quietly as you can."

They were both wearing rubber-soled shoes and made no noise as they tiptoed over the thick carpets to the green baize door in the corner. It was a swing door with no lock or latch. Nick pushed at it carefully.

Behind was a short passage and, at the end, just visible in the light from the hall, was another door. The children let the baize door swing slowly into place and then, in the darkness, felt their way to the second door. That was also a swing door. Nick, his knees still trembling, pushed it a little way open. At once a noise came to his ears: somebody was snoring!

He pushed the door wider open, and through the crack caught sight of two things: a big fat woman lying back in a wicker chair, asleep and snoring, and a flight of stairs just behind her, leading to the first floor.

He shut the door and in a whisper told Katie what he had seen.

"Shall we risk waking the woman, and make for the back stairs?" he said.

"Yes," said Katie, as her knees began to shake too. "Come on, Nick. Nothing ventured, nothing gained!"

CHAPTER 13

A Shock for Nick

Nick tiptoed round the door into the vast kitchen. The woman still snored on, her mouth open. Katie followed. The two skirted the big kitchen carefully, keeping an eye on the woman. She gave an extra loud snore and stirred in her sleep. The two children froze. They waited, holding their breath, until she once more began to snore rhythmically and then they tiptoed forward again.

Just as they crept behind her, a dreadful thing happened. Nick didn't see a cat under the woman's chair, but the cat saw him. It leaped out at him playfully, and he fell over it. Down he went, and bumped into the chair.

Katie was terrified. She was by some heavy curtains that reached to the ground. She slid behind them just as the woman jumped up heavily from the chair.

Nick was up and running for the back stairs when she saw him.

"Hey you!" the woman shouted. "What are you doing? Who are you?"

But Nick had disappeared upstairs, leaving Katie behind the curtains in the kitchen. Blow, blow, blow – what a maddening thing to happen!

The woman was too fat to chase Nick up the stairs and catch him, but she soon gave the alarm. She caught up a hand-bell from a table, and shook it vigorously.

Jangle-jangle-jangle!

Katie shivered in her hiding place. Supposing the woman saw her shape behind the curtain – she would be discovered too! What would happen next?

Plenty happened almost at once. Two men came racing out to the kitchen, shouting out something in a foreign language. They were Indians, quite small, and looked fierce. They shouted in English to the woman.

"What's the matter?" cried one man. "Why have you rung the bell?"

"A boy! He went up there!" shrieked the woman.

"You've been dreaming," suggested the other man. "No one could have got into the house."

"I saw him," said the woman indignantly. "He crashed into my chair!"

The man said something rapidly to the other man. Katie could not understand a word. Then one man sped up the back stairs and the other ran back to the hall, apparently to go up the front stairs, and so cut the boy off, wherever he was. Nobody knew that Katie was behind the curtains.

Katie stood there shaking, wondering if they would come hunting for her. Could Nick find a safe hiding place somewhere upstairs or would the men find him? It wasn't long before she knew. She heard sudden shouts from the men, and then Nick's voice.

"You let go of my arm, you beast. You're hurting me!"

Katie wanted to go to Nick's help, but what was the good of that? She would simply be taken prisoner, too. So she stayed where she was, very scared. The fat woman sank down into her wicker chair again, muttering. Katie could hear the chair creaking beneath her weight.

Upstairs, poor Nick was having a rough time. He had darted up the back stairs like a monkey and on to a small narrow landing. He had made for the first door he saw, and it had opened on to a big landing.

On the opposite side he could see another flight of stairs, wide and sweeping, which must be the front stairs, leading down into the hall. If he could slip down those, he could make his way to the garden door and escape!

But a small dark man came up the stairs just as he ran to the top. Nick darted back, straight into the arms of the man who had rushed up the back stairs. He was caught!

The two men were soon joined by two more. Three of them looked like Indians, one of whom wore a turban, and looked much more stately than the others. The fourth man seemed to be English by his looks and his speech.

"Who are you?" asked the turbaned man. Nick made no answer.

"Let's take him up to the other kids and see if they know him," said the fourth man, who spoke English well. "How did he get in? There's something funny about this."

Nick was dragged up another flight of stairs, and then to a big door. It was locked and the key was in the lock. The turbaned man turned it, and opened the door. He pushed Nick inside at once.

"Nick!" shouted two delighted voices. "Nick! You've come!"

"Shh," said Nick, afraid that the unsuspecting twins would ask where Katie was. He didn't want the men to know there had been anyone with him. The four men came round the door. The Englishman spoke to the twins.

"So he's a friend of yours, is he? Who is he? How did he know you were here?"

Nick frowned at the twins, and they guessed they were not to give him away. They looked innocently at the four frowning men.

"Didn't you tell him we were here? Perhaps Miss Twisley did. Can he stay and talk to us?"

"Pah!" said the man. He turned to one of the foreigners and spoke sharply to him. "Fetch Miss Twisley here. She may know this boy."

In two or three minutes, a sharp-faced woman came in. She eyed Nick in surprise.

"Who's he?" she said to the watching men. "Why have you brought him here?"

"Don't you know him?" asked the turbaned man. She shook her head, puzzled. Nick didn't like her at all. She had a hard, cruel face, with lips so thin that they could hardly be seen.

There was a short consultation between all five in some foreign language. Then the Englishman turned to the three waiting children.

"We shall leave you here for the night, and if you don't talk in the morning, and tell us how this boy knew you were here, you'll be very sorry, I can tell you."

The children said nothing, but watched the men go out with Miss Twisley. The door closed, the key turned in the lock. Prisoners again, but at least there were three of them now, and Katie was somewhere loose in the house!

CHAPTER 14

What Will Katie Do?

As soon as the footsteps had died away, and the children were alone, they turned eagerly to one another. Nick put his fingers to his lips. "Be careful what you say," he whispered, "one of them may have been left outside the door to listen. Look, let's go over to the window, and get behind those thick curtains, then they won't be able to hear a word."

Strange stories were exchanged behind the curtains! The twins told Nick that when Miss Lawley left, another woman had been employed to look after them. She must have been part of the kidnappers' gang because it was she who had arranged to take them away.

"We were to go on holiday somewhere lovely, so she said," whispered David. "But she wouldn't tell us where. The car came, and off we went but we were brought here instead of the somewhere lovely! We managed to overhear Miss Twisley phoning once and caught the name 'Bringking Hill', at least, that's what it sounded like, and we had to hope you would eventually get the letter that we threw out of the car."

"Yes, we did," said Nick. "And we discovered that Brinkin Hill, not Bringking as you thought, was quite near Swanage, where we've come for our holiday again. So we did a bit of snooping round on our own, and found the place, and you!"

"You're both brilliant," said Sophie. "We think we must have been given sleeping pills, or something, because we fell absolutely sound asleep in the car, and when we woke up, we were in this room! It's our bedroom, as well as our living-room. You can't imagine how awful it is to sleep, eat and play all in the same room, day after day."

Nick had already seen two beds there. A thought struck him. "How on earth did you get the key of that garden door?" he asked. "We slipped in easily with it."

"Well, Miss Twisley took us out in the grounds for a walk because we had grumbled so much at not being allowed out," said David. "We went through that outside door, of course. And when we came back, she locked it carefully behind us, but left the key in the lock! Sophie pretended to fall over the rug in the hall and hurt her knee. She yelled so frightfully that Miss Twisley took her eyes off me for a moment and I whizzed back to the door and took the key. Easy!"

"That was terrific!" said Nick, admiringly. "Are these people holding you for ransom, or something? What are they demanding? Do they want the ruby?"

"I suppose so. We don't really know," said Sophie. "Nick, where's Katie? Did she come with you? You said 'we' just now when you spoke about getting in through the garden door."

"Katie is somewhere in the house," said Nick. "She hid when I got caught. I've no idea where she is now. I only hope she'll escape before they find her. If she can give the alarm, then we'll all be rescued."

"Where can she be, I wonder?" said Sophie. "She must be scared hiding all by herself."

Katie certainly was scared. She had stood shivering behind the curtains for what seemed a very long while. The woman was still in the kitchen, so Katie didn't dare to try and escape.

Suddenly she heard footsteps coming down the little passage that led from the hall to the kitchen. The door swung open and the four men came in. The woman stood up at once.

The men snapped out some questions about Nick, but she could tell them nothing, except that she had been asleep, had been awakened by the noise of someone falling against her chair, had sprung up and seen Nick running up the back stairs.

"We shall have to take the children somewhere else immediately!" said the Englishman. "If this boy, Nick, knows enough to come here, then others may know what he knows, too. But how did he know? Well, we'll make them talk in the morning."

"Where can we hide them now, then?" asked one of the men.

The turbaned man answered at once in his own language and everyone nodded.

Katie strained her ears, but she couldn't understand what the man had said. Were they really going to take Sophie and David somewhere else, and Nick, too, this time? If only she could escape and raise the alarm!

"But by the time I've escaped, got home, and raised the alarm, these men will have whisked the others away," she thought dismally. "And I'm not sure I could get over that wall from this side without Nick's help. In fact, I'm sure I couldn't!"

She listened again to the men talking and picked up a few bits of news. Sophie and David had been kidnapped, and their ransom was the Rajah's Ruby! If the ruby was not delivered to them, according to their instructions, then the children would never be heard of again!

"And once more ill fortune will have followed the owners of the ruby," thought Katie. "Oh dear – this is like a bad dream."

She listened again. The Englishman was speaking now, half in a foreign language, and half in his own. Apparently he was urging the turbaned man to send someone to steal the ruby which, according to him, could be done, if his plan was followed.

"Time is valuable," urged the man. "If we can get the ruby at once, by doing what I suggest, then why not? What is the point of messing about with the children, and holding things up?"

"It is bad luck to steal the Rajah's Ruby," said the turbaned man. "It should always be given by one person to another. But maybe we shall have to get it your way, Williams. I do not know."

They went out of the kitchen. The fat woman muttered and groaned. She turned off the light and went mumbling up the back stairs, leaving the kitchen in darkness.

Here was Katie's chance. What, oh what, was the best thing to do?

CHAPTER 15

KATIE DOES WELL

It didn't take Katie long to make up her mind. She felt sure she wouldn't be able to climb back over the wall without Nick's helping hand and, anyway, by the time she got help it would be morning or later, and there was the chance that all three of the others would have been spirited away into thin air.

"I haven't a clue where those nasty men would take them to," thought Katie desperately. "To the other side of the world perhaps, and we might never hear of them again. I'd be the only one left – how dreadful!"

She peeped between the curtains into the dark kitchen. There was no moonlight there, and except for a glow from the cooker on which the cook had left something simmering, there was no light at all. She drew back behind the curtains as she heard the pad of footsteps in the room above.

Katie made up her mind to wait quietly till everyone had gone to bed. Then she would creep up the stairs by herself, find the room where Sophie, David and Nick were imprisoned, and let them out!

"That is, if the key's on the outside of the door still," she thought. "I don't know what I shall do if it isn't!"

She had put her watch in her rucksack when she was swimming that afternoon and had forgotten to take it out. She had no idea how late it was – half past eleven? Midnight? It could be any time. She came out from behind the curtain and wondered if there was a better hiding place. She listened intently for a few moments, but the house was wrapped in a profound silence.

She tiptoed to the door that led out to the hall, holding her breath. A pat on her ankle made her jump violently.

She rushed back to the curtains and then scolded herself. It was only that playful cat, of course! She had nearly screamed in fright when it had jumped out and patted her foot. She really must be more careful. She tiptoed to the door again, and the cat wreathed itself round her legs, asking her to play. But Katie had no time to play. In fact, she felt very cross with the cat for tripping up Nick, and causing him to be caught.

She slipped out of the door into the little passage that led to the baize door. She opened this very cautiously and peeped through the crack. The hall was quiet and deserted, lit dimly as before.

Next to the baize door was a cupboard. Katie thought it would be a good idea to creep into it. She could sit down then and have a rest, till she decided it was late enough to go and find the others.

She went into the cupboard, which was full of coats and boots. She pulled some of the coats down to the floor to lie on. Then she waited. She was tired, and everything was very quiet. The coats were soft. Katie's eyes closed, her head fell forward, and she slept peacefully.

She awoke with a jump. Somehow the cat had followed her. It had made its way into the cupboard by inserting its paw into the crack of the door and then wriggling itself through. Purring loudly, it was now on Katie's knee, pushing its claws in and out of her jeans. She was wide awake at once and, luckily, did not cry out.

"Oh, it's you again," she whispered to the cat. "Stop digging your claws into me – but thank you for waking me. How long have I been asleep?" She pushed the cat off her jeans and it ran out of the cupboard and back into the kitchen, easing its way through the baize door.

Katie crept out of the cupboard into the hall. The light had been left on but there was not a sound to be heard anywhere. It felt very late, she thought. Actually it was about two o'clock and she had slept for over two hours.

She went softly up the wide stairs, and came out on to a landing. The air was heavy and muggy. Katie was damp with perspiration, but whether this was caused by the heat or her own fear, she wasn't sure. All was quiet. No lights were to be seen anywhere, except from the hall below. Katie cautiously switched on her torch.

Up she went again to the second floor, trying to make out on which side of the house the twins' room should be. She came to a door and, flashing her torch quickly round, she caught sight of a piece of paper sticking out from beneath the bottom edge of one of the doors facing her.

She remembered Sophie had said in her message that they would mark their room in that way. They had remembered, and here was the mark. This must be the right room.

Luckily, the key was on her side of the door. If only, only it was the right door! She bent down and tried to see if there was a light shining through the keyhole, but of course the key was in it and she could see nothing. She didn't dare to take it out, in case it rattled.

She tried the door cautiously. It was locked. She turned the key. It squeaked a little and she stood still in fright. But nobody came; nobody called out!

She unlocked the door completely, and turned the handle. She opened the door and slipped swiftly round it, shutting it quietly behind her.

A voice at once spoke from the darkness of the room. "Who's that?"

It was Nick's voice. Katie could have cried with joy.

"It's me, Katie," she whispered. "I've unlocked the door. Are Sophie and David here? Let's be quick and get out before anyone comes!"

"The twins are asleep," came Nick's low voice. "I didn't let myself sleep, I was so hoping you might come. Good old Katie! We'll wake the twins and escape."

Nick switched on his little torch. He woke the twins quietly and they sat up at once.

"Katie's here," whispered Nick. "She's unlocked the door from the outside. Let's go quickly. We're all dressed, so we don't need to wait for anything."

Shaking with excitement and delight, the twins went to the door with Nick and Katie. They stood outside on the landing for a moment listening, and then Nick led the way very cautiously.

"Go downstairs carefully, but watch out for the cat," he whispered. "Then we'll leave by the garden door. Now, not a sound, anyone. Come on!"

CHAPTER 16

ESCAPE TO THE ISLAND

The four children went softly along the landing and came to the head of the stairs. They went down, glad that there was such a thick carpet to muffle their footsteps. They were soon on the first floor.

Then down to the hall they crept. Nick led the way to the garden door, wondering whether the men had discovered that they had left the key on the outside.

They apparently hadn't, but they had bolted the door inside, so someone had evidently found that it was unlocked and, not having been able to find the key, had drawn the bolts.

It took only a matter of a second or two to unbolt the door and slip out. The moon was still bright, though in the south-west some big banked-up clouds were gathering and the atmosphere was very close.

"It's going to pour soon," said Nick. "It

looks like there's a storm coming – and listen, that's thunder, isn't it?"

"Yes," said Katie, as she heard a rumble. "We can't go scrambling over the countryside at night in a storm, especially as we have only got two bicycles. I think we'd better go down to the island on the secret lake for the rest of the night. We can put up our tent and nobody will ever guess we're there."

Nick thought it was a good idea. They were all tired out with excitement and strain, and longing to rest and sleep. So, without more discussion, they made their way to the wall, climbed over and then struggled down the steep hill, glad of the moon to light the way. They jumped into the little boat and paddled sleepily off to the island.

"This boat's leaking," said Sophie, feeling her feet suddenly wet.

"It's because there are four of us and we're heavy," said Nick, though Katie couldn't see why weight should make the boat leak. But she was too tired to argue, and hardly felt the water coming into her shoes as she and Nick paddled valiantly across to the little island.

They heard a clap of thunder as they landed, and it made them all jump. "Look at that enormous black cloud coming up," said Sophie. "It will soon blot out the moon. I think there's going to be a terrific storm. We'll get soaked. Is there anywhere to shelter on the island?"

A large drop of rain struck Nick on the head. Then another and another. Yes, they would definitely all get soaked! He thought of the strange little temple with its silent figures. Could they shelter there?

"Katie, do you think we'd better climb through that unfastened window into the temple where those statues are?" he asked. "I can't see that it would matter if we sheltered there. Nobody seems to bother about the place now. Those men probably don't even know it's here."

The black cloud suddenly swept over the moon and at once everywhere was dark. Nick switched on his torch.

"Better take the rug and the sleeping-bags and the food and everything into the temple too," he said. "They'll all be soaked if we don't."

The wind got up and blew loudly. More rain came, spiteful rain that stung their faces and hands. Hurriedly they collected everything from the little clearing and ran to the strange building.

"Shelter in the porch till I climb in at the window and open the door," said Nick. So they stood there, shivering, while he clambered in through the swinging window and went round to the door.

But he couldn't open the door, and had to open a big window nearby instead. The others passed all the food and various belongings through to Nick, and then climbed into the temple themselves. Nick flashed his torch round the room. The twins exclaimed in surprise at the sight of the large seated figures.

"Whatever are those weird statues? I don't think I like them," said Sophie. "Gosh – have we got to sleep with them smiling and staring at us all the time?"

"They won't hurt us," said Katie. "I think they're statues of Indian gods! Wow! Listen to the storm now! I'm glad we didn't try to battle all the way back in this. We'd never have got there!"

"I'm going to light this funny little oil lamp," said Nick, who had found a boat-shaped one on a table. "That's if it still has oil in. Yes, it has. Good. The moon's gone for the night and a little light on the scene will cheer things up."

But it didn't really. It just made the statues look horribly lifelike, because the light flickered on their jewelled eyes and made them gleam and shine.

"Not very nice company," said Nick, flinging himself down on a sleeping-bag. "Come on, everyone. Let's lie down and try and get a bit of sleep!"

Katie found a few mats to make the floor softer, but the children were all very uncomfortable indeed. Nobody could go to sleep, especially as the wind howled round like a mad thing, and draughts blew in everywhere. Great torrents of rain beat against the roof, and the thunder rumbled round.

The lightning flashed now and again revealing the jewel-eyed statues. Everyone felt uneasy and longed for dawn to break. They were all damp and shivering with only two sleeping-bags between them.

The oil lamp flickered and went out. There had been very little oil in it. Now it was quite dark except for an occasional flash of lightning. But gradually the storm died away, and the wind blew less strongly.

It was in a quiet moment that Nick heard a strange noise. What could it be? It came from somewhere outside.

He sat up, listening, then he got up and went to the window. In a moment, he'd recognised the sound. Someone was rowing a boat and it was the sound of oars that he had heard, of course it was! Had they been discovered? Who was coming?

He roused the others, who were half dozing. "Someone's coming," he said. "I can hear the oars. They mustn't find us here, or our belongings! Quick, we must hide them – and hide ourselves, too!"

CHAPTER 17

A SECRET VISIT

The others were wide awake at once, and Katie looked round the strange room, scared. She couldn't at first remember where she was. The storm had passed, and the night was no longer absolutely dark as dawn had lightened its black to grey. The silent statues loomed over the children, the brightness of their eyes lost in the shadows.

They all heard the click of the oars in the rowlocks of a boat.

"Who can it be?" whispered Sophie.

"I can only think it's one or more of the men from Brinkin Towers, come to hunt for us," said Nick desperately. "They must have discovered we'd gone, and begun to search for us. I don't know why they should think we'd come here! Perhaps they found their boat gone, and that made them suspicious."

"Oh, no! They're bound to see it now," said Katie. "They'll probably land in the same cove as we did! They'll know for certain we're here, then."

"I wonder where they got the second boat from," said Nick. "I only saw the old one, which we took."

"They'd be sure to have a good boat somewhere," David said. "They wouldn't use that dirty decaying one for themselves."

"I was so hoping that they didn't know about this island," said Katie. "Now we'll all be prisoners if they find us."

The children heard the sound of voices. Nick leaped up.

"They'll search this building," he said. "Let's see if there's anywhere to hide. We might as well give them a run for their money. Make them hunt about a bit!"

"Look, let's put everything under that great table," said Sophie. "We can drape the cloth over our things and hide them."

"And do you see those heavy gold curtains up there behind the big, smiling idol, the one sitting high on that platform arrangement?" said Nick. "We could all stand behind them. Come on, let's hurry! I can hear the boat being pulled up now; they'll be with us in a minute."

There was no sound of footsteps, but they heard the voices much more clearly now, though they couldn't make out the words. Katie and Sophie put everything under the big table, and then dragged down the heavy cloth that covered it, so that it hid what was underneath.

The boys were exploring behind the curtains. "Come on," they called to the girls. "The curtains are woven loosely, leaving little holes patterned with embroidery which we can see through without being seen. Hurry up!"

Just as the sound of a key turning came from the door at the front of the temple, the two girls climbed up to the little platform, and slipped behind the heavy gold curtain. They saw at once that what the boys had said was true: they could peer through the tiny holes embroidered in the material.

A voice came loudly to their ears. "Bring the things in here, Amar."

It was the voice of the Englishman called Williams whom they had seen with the Indians. Each of the children put an eye to a hole in the curtains, and watched silently as two men came into the room.

A little dark man, whom they hadn't seen before, came in with Williams. He was dressed in loose robes, and glanced round at the great statues in fright and awe. Williams took no notice of them whatsoever.

The children braced themselves, expecting the men to search for them. But they didn't! The two men were not looking for them at all. Instead they did some very strange things indeed.

The little man, evidently a servant of some kind, carried what looked like a roll of thick cloth over his shoulder. He set it down, and Williams helped to unroll it. The children, at the holes in the curtain, tried their hardest to see what was happening.

The roll of cloth appeared to be three rugs of some kind. They were laid out on the floor. The little servant disappeared, and came back with a box that appeared to be extremely heavy. He put it down with a thud that shook the room.

"Everything in there?" asked Williams, and opened the lid. "Fetch the other box and let me have a look at that."

Another box was brought and put down with a thud. It was duly examined and the lid shut down again. Williams looked round the strange room with its curious idols, carved swords and beautiful vases.

"These must be worth a load of money," he said. "My word – look at that grinning, cross-legged creature up there on the platform!"

This was the figure just in front of the curtain behind which the children were hiding. They shrank back as the man came near to the platform. He shone his torch on the face of the glittering statue.

"What have you got to laugh at, sitting there day and night alone in this horrible place?" demanded Williams. The little dark servant pulled at his sleeve nervously, evidently disapproving of such behaviour. He muttered something in a strange language. The Englishman laughed.

"You're not really afraid of him, are you, Amar? Like to see me topple him over?"

Filled with real horror at such an idea, the Indian turned and ran out of the room. Williams followed, laughing. In amazement, the children heard the door being shut, and after a while, the sound of the boat being rowed off again over the water.

"Why didn't they look for us?" said Nick, bewildered.

"Why did they come here with all that stuff, whatever it is?" asked Sophie. "And what is the stuff? Let's go and see, now we're safe."

They all stepped down from the platform to the ground. The first rays of the rising sun shone on the things the men had brought.

"Look at all this!" said Nick, astounded. "How very – very – extraordinary!"

CHAPTER 18

Unexpected Gifts – and a Shock

The two men had certainly left some puzzling things in the little temple. The children stood and looked at them in surprise.

"Three thick, warm rugs, each big enough to roll round anyone two or three times," said David, astonished.

"A box of tinned food – all kinds!" said Katie, lifting the lid.

"And in here are bottles," exclaimed Sophie, looking into the second big box.

"What are they all for?" wondered David. "Is someone coming to camp out here?"

"Oh, I know what it is!" said Nick suddenly. "They haven't discovered yet that we've escaped, but they're making their plans for moving us out of Brinkin Towers and they've decided to hide us here, in this peculiar temple, or whatever it is!"

The others stared at him, the girls' faces pale with horror. Then David smacked him on the back and laughed.

"You've got it, Nick! Hey, would you believe it, the kidnappers have picked on the same place to dump us that we ourselves have chosen to hide in! I call that really funny."

Everyone laughed. They felt suddenly much more cheerful. So their escape hadn't yet been discovered, and even when it was discovered, the men wouldn't think of searching in the very place they themselves had prepared.

"These things they've brought are supposed to be for us, when they get us here!" grinned Nick. "Three rugs, because, of course, they thought there were only three of us as they haven't seen Katie, and food enough to last for days. It's brilliant!"

"Looking at those tins has made me feel hungry," said Sophie. "What about having a snack now? And I'm frightfully thirsty, too."

"Okay. We'll have a good tuck-in at the food our enemies have so kindly provided us with," said Nick. "And then, instead of tossing and turning and shivering with only two sleeping-bags between us, we'll have a really comfortable sleep in the great thick rugs those fellows have given us out of the kindness of their hearts! I'm going to enjoy all this!"

"And when we wake up, we'll take our boat and row to the other end of the lake, find a landing place somewhere, and make our way home," said Sophie. "And we'll send the police after those rogues. This is a very nice adventure indeed now."

"Don't count your chickens before they're hatched," said David warningly. "You're always doing that, Sophie. It may not be so easy as you think. Once those fellows know we've escaped, they'll search everywhere. We'll have to be on our guard."

"Oh, we're all right now. Don't be such a pessimist!" said Sophie. "Anyone got a tin-opener?"

They were soon eating ham, hacked out of a tin with a penknife, and biscuits and tinned peaches, washed down with lemonade.

"I wish the men had provided Coca-Cola instead of lemonade, but otherwise this is just about the nicest meal I've ever had," said Sophie. "It's all the better because we're eating it sitting on the floor, surrounded by those strange figures, in the very early morning before anyone else is up!"

"It's seven o'clock right now," said David, his mouth full. "People will soon be up and about!" He yawned hugely. "Oh, I am tired. I'll be able to sleep properly now, in those thick rugs with a good meal inside me."

The rugs were certainly very big and cosy and the floor didn't feel nearly so hard. It didn't take long for all four children to fall fast asleep, tired out with the night's excitement. They slept till the sun was high in the sky.

David woke first, and lay for a minute or two, looking straight into the face of one of the statues that seemed to be watching him. He sat up and laughed.

"Are you thinking it's strange to have four visitors for the night?" he asked the silent figure. "What's the time? Hey, it's almost half past ten, and what a fantastic morning it is!" He woke up the others, and they all sat up, trying to remember where they were.

"I'm still sleepy," yawned Katie. "What a lovely day! Let's go and have a swim in the lake before breakfast. Do you think it's safe to do that, Nick?"

"Oh yes. We'll find a sheltered spot where nobody looking out from Brinkin Towers could see us," said Nick. "Then we'll have breakfast, find our boat, and see if we can make for the other side of the lake and get home from there."

They left the temple and ran down to the little cove. They looked for their boat, wondering again how it was that the men hadn't spotted it the night before.

They soon knew why it hadn't been discovered. It wasn't there. They stared about, puzzled and bewildered. Where could the boat be?

"Did anyone tie it up?" asked Nick, trying to remember. "No, nobody did; we just pulled it up on the sand. The storm must have swept it away. We'll have to look for it."

They began a silent, rather depressed search for the boat. Nick and Katie walked round one side of the island and Sophie and David hunted round the other side. It was nowhere to be seen on the shallow edge of the lake nor could anyone see a sign of it floating in the deeper water. David found it at last and called the others. He pointed sadly into the deep water off the east side of the island.

"There's the boat," he said. "Sunk to the bottom, with just the floating paddles marking where it went down. You remember it was leaking badly. Well, I suppose the storm took it round here, and it filled and sank."

No one said a word. This wasn't good at all. Now, with their boat gone, they had no way of escape from the island. What a dreadful disappointment!

CHAPTER 19

PRISONERS AGAIN!

It really was a terrible blow to find their boat sunk. The two boys swam out and dived down to it but it was quite impossible for them to raise it up, the water was too deep. Nick gave a sigh.

"Bang go our beautiful plans!" he said at last. "We've escaped from Brinkin Towers to this island, only to find we're prisoners here!" Dejectedly, the two boys swam back to the waiting girls who were both very upset to hear that there was no way to leave the island.

"I suppose it's too far to swim across the lake?" asked David hopefully.

"I think so," said Nick. "Too far for Katie, anyway. She certainly can't swim that far. Can you, Sophie?"

"I might be able to, but it's a really long way and I'd be a bit scared to try," said Sophie. "Anyway, even if we three could swim, we can't leave Katie here on her own. If the men found her, they'd just use her as a hostage." They stared at one another gloomily.

"This kind of thing always happens when you count your silly chickens," said David crossly, scowling at poor Sophie. "I warned you early this morning."

"That's got nothing to do with it," said Sophie. "It did seem as if things were going right then, you know it did!"

They decided to have a swim, even though they felt very gloomy. It was a good idea. After a little splashing and giggling they all felt much better. They clambered out, hungry and glowing.

They made a very good second breakfast of some tinned sardines, and more biscuits, finishing up with pineapple chunks and some tinned cream.

"Excellent," said David. "I can't think why people don't always have meals like this. As for pineapple chunks, I really believe I could go on eating them all day long – so sweet and squishy and pineapply."

"Idiot," said Sophie. "You're just plain greedy, that's all."

"Let's have a talk about things," said Nick, when they had finished. "We ought to make some sort of plan. I haven't got any ideas at all, though."

"What do you suppose the men up in Brinkin Towers are doing now they've missed us?" asked David. "Miss Twisley would have gone in to wake us about a quarter to eight. It's almost midday now. We'll have been missed for some hours."

"They'll wonder how we got out through a locked door," said Sophie, grinning.

"I imagine they'll have searched the house thoroughly, to begin with," said Nick. "After that they would search the grounds and probably find where we got over the wall, and then begin to hunt everywhere."

"Do you suppose they would think that we'd come to this island?" asked Katie anxiously.

Nick thought for a moment, then he shook his head. "No, I don't think so. They've probably completely forgotten about that old, ruined boathouse and the mouldering boat."

"They didn't see it here last night, either,

because it had sunk," said Sophie. "Unless they thought of us swimming here, but I doubt if it would enter their heads that we might be in the temple, and swimming wouldn't be very likely!"

"You're right. The island is a good way from the mainland," said David. "And it would have meant swimming at night. No, they won't guess we're here. Anyway, I don't think it would occur to them that we are actually in the very place they planned to imprison us themselves, especially as two of them brought the rugs and the food over here early this morning. I think we're pretty safe from discovery."

"Who's counting their chickens now?" demanded Sophie. But David took no notice of her.

"It looks as if we're in for a fairly long camping holiday!" he went on, with rather a shaky laugh.

"We've got plenty of food," said Nick. "But it won't last for ever. Anyway, if things begin to look dangerous, I'll have a shot at swimming across the lake. I could get my bike and make my way back to our house somehow."

"They'll have found our bikes by now, I expect," said Katie suddenly. "Blow!"

"That'll puzzle them!" said Nick, with a grin. "Two bikes! They'll be really worried. Who owns the second and where is he?"

"She, you mean," said Katie. "They'll see mine's a girl's bike. Won't they be furious! They'll wonder where I am, and maybe guess I had something to do with letting you all out of that locked room."

"They'd be right," said Sophie, finishing the last of her lemonade. "Well, we may as well enjoy this unexpected camping holiday. But what about your mother, Nick, won't she be worried about you?"

"No, because she's had to go up to help Aunt Jill who's hurt her leg, and she knows we're camping out for a few days," explained Nick.

"We told her about your being up here and said we were coming to see you," added Katie. "We didn't say you'd been kidnapped of course! She's quite happy for us to be with you."

"We must try and escape somehow," said Nick. "Mum said she'd only be away for three or four days, and I'd hate her to get back and worry about why we haven't phoned and where we've got to."

"She'd certainly be very concerned if she knew the mess we're in," said David thoughtfully. "You and I may have to swim across, Nick, and leave the girls hidden here."

Nick was quite glad that they weren't going to try this straight away, as privately he wondered whether he would be able to swim as far as the mainland. He sat back with a sigh.

That first day was rather peculiar. Nobody could quite get used to the idea that although they were apparently on holiday, actually they were prisoners on the island. True, nobody knew they were prisoners except themselves, but they were, all the same. Unless someone took them off in a boat, there they would have to stay!

"I keep feeling all happy and carefree and giggly," said Sophie, "and then I suddenly remember we can't get away, and it depresses me so much I feel really miserable."

"Oh, you'll get used to it after a few weeks," said David.

Sophie looked so alarmed at his remark that they all laughed. She gave her brother a thump. "You're counting the wrong sort of chickens!" she said. "I'd love this for a few days, but not for ever! Not even for three weeks."

"It may come to that," said Nick soberly. "We must be sensible and face up to things. We're in a fix, you know, and I'm not sure that after today we oughtn't to begin to ration out the food a bit!"

What a very nasty thought! They all fell on poor Nick and pummelled him for his alarming speech, but secretly, of course, they knew he was right. They were in a fix.

CHAPTER 20

No Way of Escape

And so the four children's strange kind of holiday continued. They couldn't get away from the little island, but they had delicious food and drink, and at night, if the weather was warm and fine, they lay outside wrapped in sleeping-bags and rugs or, if it was cooler, they slept inside the temple.

They could paddle and swim to their heart's content, and race about all day long if they wanted to. Yet it wasn't like a proper holiday.

"We've always got to be on the look-out in case anyone comes," complained David. "And we've always to be careful not to shout too loudly for fear we're heard."

"We daren't light a fire either because the smoke would be seen," said Katie. "I'd really like some hot soup or baked beans if the evening is chilly."

"I know. It spoils things," said Sophie.

"And how long have we been here now? I'm afraid we'll lose track of the days if we stay here too long."

"No, we won't," said Nick, showing them a stick. "Look, I'm making a notch for each night we spend here. Two notches so far – and I'll make the next one tonight."

By that evening, the children had explored every inch of the island. They had been able to make out the plan of the garden designed around the temple where they found traces of old rose beds, flowering shrubs and strange trees. They had thought about trying to weed the beds and uncover the paths, but anyone coming to search the island would certainly notice that people had been there recently.

The children took it in turns to sit opposite the path leading up to Brinkin Towers, watching in case anyone came down to the lakeside. On the first afternoon, David saw the men searching the undergrowth against the wall round the house, but no one had even glanced over to the island. Nick and Katie wondered whether their two bicycles had been discovered, tucked well into the bushes.

The next morning, Sophie saw four of the men setting off down the steep hill to Brinkin village and returning very slowly and out of breath a couple of hours later.

Nick was on duty that afternoon, lying in the sunshine by the lake. As he watched some moorhens swimming in the shallow water, a flash of colour caught his attention. He froze, pressing himself into the sand and turning his head slowly sideways. It was Amar, the Indian who had brought the food to the temple the first morning, and it was his scarlet robe that he had seen.

Nick whistled softly, "*Tui-tui-tui-too,*" the signal they had agreed to use as a warning if someone appeared.

Amar stood at the top of the path just outside the gate set into the wall of Brinkin Towers. He was staring fixedly at the island.

"Has he seen somebody here?" thought Nick. "I don't think he can see me, but I don't know where everyone else is."

The other three children had heard Nick's whistle. They weren't far away from the temple but they couldn't be seen from the lake because of the thick trees.

"What do you think Nick has seen?"

whispered Katie. "Should we hide in case someone's coming?"

"No," said David. "We'll creep as close as we can to the beach, keeping to the trees and the bushes, and see what's happening. Come on, and don't say a word."

Amar still stood at the top of the path. Then he began to walk slowly down the steps to the lakeside. He half stumbled on a broken paving stone and Nick quickly rolled over to the safety of the nearest bush.

"Psst!" whispered David from another bush close by. "What's happening?"

Nick told him quickly. "The best thing to do is to stay hidden and silent here," he said. "We haven't seen any boat on the other side of the lake, so I don't think Amar can get across here."

Amar reached the lakeside and again stood still. Nick realised that his eyes were focused on the little temple and he was not interested in the rest of the island. A sudden shout made Amar turn and start back up the stone steps.

The angry voice called to him again, and he hurried up to the top of the path and in through the gate.

The children waited a few minutes and then crawled thankfully out of the bushes.

"What do you think Amar was doing, Nick?" asked Sophie. "Do you think he was looking for us?"

"I don't know," answered Nick. "He didn't seem to be looking at anything except the temple."

"I'm glad he didn't have a boat over the other side of the lake," said Katie. "What would we have done if he'd rowed across here?"

"I think he would have gone straight to the temple," said David thoughtfully. "If he does come, we'd probably be safest in the bushes."

"Let's go and get some food," said Nick. "Being scared always makes me hungry."

"Good idea," said Sophie, standing up. "Anyway, he won't come back tonight, so we don't have to worry now."

CHAPTER 21

A VISITOR TO THE TEMPLE

It was a very warm evening and the children went swimming as the first stars came out. The moon rose, lighting a silver path across the water. It was very peaceful and very beautiful as they went back into the little temple. They lay on the thick rugs and sleeping-bags, talking softly together, hardly aware of the great statues staring down at them.

Much later, the children lay deep asleep in the darkness. No one heard the sound of quiet footsteps outside. Not until the front door opened and shut did anyone wake up.

Then Nick awoke with a jump. He sat up, scared, and poked the others quickly. They were lying in the same room as before, and there was no time to get up and hide.

"Someone's in the temple," whispered Nick in David's ear. David already knew;

he had heard quiet, padding footsteps in the passage beyond, but whoever had made them had gone into a smaller room, a room where only three carved figures sat, silent and forbidding.

A muttering sound came from the room, then a low chanting, followed by a kind of wailing song. It really scared the listening children.

"Who is it? What is he doing?" whispered Sophie. "I daren't get up to see."

Nick was the only one who dared to move. He slipped his sleeping-bag aside and without a single sound rose to his bare feet. He tiptoed across the floor to the door and stood there.

A light shone in the little room beyond the passage. The chanting and muttering came from there. Nick squeezed into the passage, not even daring to open the door a little wider in case it squeaked.

He came to the door of the little room. He peered through the crack.

What a strange sight he saw! A small Indian was on his knees before a statue, knocking his forehead against the floor as he chanted strange words to music that sounded like nothing Nick had ever heard before.

He had placed a small, boat-shaped lamp at the feet of the brooding figure and, as the light caught it, it seemed almost as if the eyes of the statue were alive. They were ruby-red, and glowed like fire.

Then the Indian rose to his feet, muttering solemnly. Nick craned his neck to see what he was going to do, but it was difficult to make out anything in the dim light. The Indian seemed to be touching the forehead of the carved figure.

He looked round suddenly as if he had sensed that Nick was watching. In fear the boy drew back, hoping he had not been seen. He tiptoed to the others, and whispered into David's ear what had been going on.

"I don't think the Indian knows anyone is here," whispered Nick. "If we don't make a sound he may go away without looking into this room."

"Couldn't we go and sit cross-legged behind that group of figures over there?" whispered David. "Then, if he did come in, he'd see nothing but a mass of figures all

sitting cross-legged together."

"Yes, that's a good idea," said Nick. "I'll tell the girls."

Very quietly indeed the four of them rose to their feet, hid all their bedding, and went behind the silent crowd of images, which were all set up as if in a museum.

They sat themselves down cross-legged, and waited there, their hearts beating far too loudly.

"Like pistons," thought Nick, trying to breathe slowly so that his heart would slow down a little. But, at a noise outside the door, it began to beat twice as quickly – thump-thump, thump-thump, thump-thump.

Someone was looking into the room, someone holding a little boat-shaped lamp, someone whose clothes were dripping wet! How still the four children sat – as still as the carved figures that surrounded them!

The man with the lamp gazed for what seemed a very long time at the crowd of cross-legged figures. Sophie thought suddenly that this would be just the moment when one of them wanted to sneeze.

No sooner had she thought that than she

felt a little movement from David, beside her. Poor David! To his extreme horror he had felt a sneeze coming. He stopped breathing. He pressed his lips tightly together. He didn't dare to hold his nose, for that would mean raising his arm.

"WHOOOOOOOSHOO!"

David was famous for his sneezes, but this was a really outsize one, a most magnificent specimen. It not only startled David; it startled the other three children, too.

But it startled the watching man most of all! He gave a loud howl and dropped his lamp to the ground, where it promptly went out. He took to his heels and fled down the passage to the front door, still howling in utter panic.

The door slammed and the children heard running footsteps, and then the sound of a tremendous splash as the little Indian dived into the lake.

Nick almost fell off the table he was sitting on, he was laughing so much.

"Oh, David," he gasped, "what a sneeze! I almost ran for the door, too!"

Sophie and Katie howled with laughter

and relief. Katie mopped her streaming eyes.

"You made me jump out of my skin, David," she said, half crying and half laughing. "Did you do it on purpose? You scared that man into the middle of next week!"

David grinned feebly. He had given himself a terrible shock, for he had really thought that the sneeze would give the whole show away. But it hadn't. It had simply scared the man off.

"He must have thought one of those statues had caught a cold or something," he said, and began to laugh thankfully. "I tried to keep the sneeze back, but it only made it all the bigger when it did come."

"Good thing too," said Nick. "You certainly frightened off the enemy. I wonder what he came for, he looked to me as if he was praying to that image in the other room. He must have swum across – he was soaking wet! Do you suppose it's safe to go to sleep again?"

David thought it was, but it was some-time before everyone dozed off. Sophie kept breaking out into giggles and that made everyone wide awake again.

"I'm hungry," said Nick. "Let's take some tins of fruit and cream and eat it outside."

"Brilliant!" giggled Sophie. "We once had a midnight feast at school in the cloakroom. It will be much more fun to have one by a lake in the moonlight!"

"We'd better whisper," said Katie, when they were sitting on the sandy beach. "Voices carry so over water."

They thoroughly enjoyed their midnight meal. David went and fetched the bedding.

"Let's sleep out here tonight," he said. "I don't much want to go back into the temple."

They lay down and looked up at the starry sky. Katie gave a huge yawn and rolled over. Very soon they were all asleep for the second time that night and this time nothing disturbed them.

CHAPTER 22

THE ENEMY AGAIN

In the morning, when the children woke up, warmed by the early sun, they wondered, for a moment, where they were. Immediately they remembered the visitor of the previous night.

"You know, I think the Indian who was here last night was Amar, the servant who came with Williams to bring the rugs and food," said Nick. "It was difficult to see him in the dim light, but I saw him yesterday afternoon staring at the temple. Our visitor last night was about the same size and wore a scarlet robe like Amar had on."

"I think you're right, Nick," said Katie. "I only saw him when we were sitting amongst the statues, but he definitely looked like Amar."

"Perhaps the statues come from Indian temples," said Sophie thoughtfully. "And Amar came to worship them. He must have hated Williams laughing at them the other night."

"I don't think Amar will come here again," said David. "He was too frightened. Let's go back to the temple and see if he left anything in that small room. He might have brought more food."

"Why should he leave food?" asked Nick sensibly. "Statues don't need to eat and none of our enemies know that we are living here."

The children took their bedding back to the temple and put it in the room where they usually slept. Then they went into the smaller room but there was nothing there. All Amar had left were tiny pools of water on the floor.

They looked at the figures in the little room. They were more finely carved than the others in the temple, and more richly dressed. One image had emerald green eyes, one had sapphire blue eyes, and the biggest one had ruby red eyes.

"I don't suppose all their jewels and rings and their eyes, too, are real precious stones, are they?" asked Katie. "I mean – I expect they would be if they were in proper temples in their own country, but these are only for show, aren't they? Sort of museum figures?"

"Oh yes, none of the jewels can possibly be real," said Nick. "Why, these figures would be worth thousands of pounds if their jewels were genuine. Look at this one's eyes; if those were really emerald, they would be worth an absolute fortune."

Sophie was looking at the biggest statue, the one with ruby red eyes. "Would our Rajah's Ruby be as big as these red stones in this figure's eyes?" she asked. "What odd eyes it has hasn't it? They don't match. One stone is bigger than the other."

"Oh, come along! Don't let's start staring at these cross-legged statues," said Nick. "They give me the creeps. I'm always expecting them to uncross their legs one night and get up and walk over to us, when we are lying asleep."

"What a horrible thought," said Katie, alarmed. "Why ever did you tell us that? Now I shan't dare to go to sleep at night."

Nick laughed. "Nothing stops you from going to sleep," he said. "Anyway, it's only a joke. Now, who's for a swim – and then what about opening a tin of sliced peaches?"

It was on the afternoon of that day that something else happened. They were snoozing in the sun, after a very good meal, all out of tins, of course, when David woke with a jump. Surely he had heard something?

He certainly had. A boat was coming swiftly to the island, a boat with four men in it: the three Indians, including the one with the turban, and also the dour-faced Englishman called Williams. All looked very fierce and angry.

"He must be there," Williams said. "He can swim like a fish. He swam all the way over, and he's there still, I'm sure! The rat – double-crossing us like that!"

David gave Nick a hefty poke. "Nick! A boatful of men are coming over here. Look!"

Nick came to with a jump and stared out over the lake. The girls were wide awake now, looking in horror at the rapidly approaching boat.

"There's no time to do anything!" whispered Nick. "Creep behind those bushes, quickly, everybody."

They all slid behind some thick bushes and lay there, as still as mice. The men had not come back to look for them, so they must be after that strange little man who had come muttering and chanting the night before, his clothes dripping wet.

The four men pulled their boat up on to the beach and, without looking round, went swiftly to the temple.

"David," whispered Nick. "I think we'll have time to shin up that enormous tree. We'd be much safer hidden up there. Come on."

The four children had never climbed a tree so quickly in their lives. They peered down from the safety of its branches. Would the men search the island when they found that the man they were looking for was not in the temple?

"They won't find Amar anywhere here at all," whispered Nick. "He was so frightened at David's sneeze that he leaped into the lake and swam off at once. We heard him!"

"It isn't likely they'll look for us if they're looking for him, then," said David thankfully.

"I don't know. They'll find the opened tins and the scattered bedding inside the temple," said Nick soberly. "They'll feel a bit puzzled, to say the least."

"It depends how desperate they are to find Amar, whether or not they think of us when they notice the tins," said Sophie.

"Maybe they'll think the missing man has been using the place for a few days," said Katie hopefully.

The men came out of the temple after a time. They were not at all pleased that they couldn't find him.

"He's not there," said the Englishman in disgust. "Maybe he's hiding somewhere on the island, then. Separate out and work your way round and inwards."

The island was not very big, and it didn't take long to go all round it. The men came back to where they had started from, looking angry and puzzled. They actually came to stand under the very tree where the children were hiding!

"He must have been here plenty of times," said one man. "He's obviously eaten out of those tins. The double-crossing toad!"

They discussed the matter both in English and in a foreign language. They slipped from one language to another in a very bewildering way and the children could not understand half that was said. Fortunately, the men never once looked up into the tree and they moved off at last. Then they stopped once more.

"We'll go round the place again," said one of the men. "I've a feeling there's someone here and if it's Amar we'll get him!" The others nodded their agreement.

Nick parted the leaves anxiously to see where the men were going. They were apparently setting off to the other side of the island. He turned his face to David, and the look on it was so excited that David was astonished.

"What's the matter?" he asked in a whisper.

"I've got an idea, David," whispered Nick exultantly. "A truly fantastic, marvellous idea!"

CHAPTER 23

THE GREAT ESCAPE

"David, this is our chance to escape! We'll shin down the tree quickly and rush for the boat," whispered Nick. "Tell the girls, and then follow me. Quick! Hurry!"

David passed the message to the girls and in seconds all four children had scrambled down the tree. Katie grazed the skin off one leg, but didn't even notice the pain. They were making for the boat that was drawn up in the cove when a shout suddenly rang out across the island.

"Hey! Look, there are the kids! Well, of all the—! Hey, stop, you kids! Look at them, they've got the boat!"

The four men were racing towards the children. Katie, Sophie and David were already in the boat and Nick shoved it off into the water. This boat had oars, and he and David each snatched one quickly. The boat glided smoothly away.

The four men reached the cove just too late. They were shouting all kinds of things in what sounded like half a dozen different languages, and two of them were shaking their fists so fiercely that they seemed almost comical. One stooped down and picked up a large stone.

He sent it skimming through the air. It struck the side of the boat with a bang and made the girls jump.

"Lie down in the boat, girls," Nick commanded. "Pull harder, David, we must get out of range. The brutes!"

Another stone hit the boat, and a third fell into the water nearby. A fourth one hit David's oar and made him jump.

"Row harder!" urged Nick fiercely. "One of us will be hit!"

At last, after what seemed an hour or two, but was really only a few minutes, they were out of range of the stones. The boys did not relax though, they rowed as if their lives depended on it, and it was only when David fell across his oar in exhaustion that Nick called a halt.

The girls sat up, looking very scared.

"We're safe now," said Nick, out of breath. "It was a near thing, though."

"Anyway, we've escaped," said Katie thankfully. Her face suddenly brightened and she looked at Nick with shining eyes.

"Nick! Nick! Who are prisoners now on that island? The four men! They've no boat, and unless they're brilliant swimmers, they can't get back to the mainland."

Everyone began to laugh out of sheer relief. It was wonderful to think that the men were now going to have a taste of being prisoners on the island!

Nick began to row again. "Take your oar, David," he said. "We must get across the lake at once and call the police. They can capture those four men – no problem at all – and the others in Brinkin Towers, too, because none of them will know that the other four are prisoners on the island!"

"Hey! What a scoop!" said David, pulling at his oar, with Katie helping him. "It was a real brainwave of yours, Nick, getting this boat!"

It seemed a long way across the lake, because they deliberately made for the shore furthest from the island in case any of the Brinkin Towers men were along the banks of the lake. They landed at last, pulling the boat up into the bank where the water was shallow.

"Now to make our way through these thick woods," said Nick, leading the way. "And all I hope is we don't lose ourselves, and that we come out somewhere sensible!"

"Yes – where there's a proper telephone," agreed David, forcing back a whole mass of brambles.

"What a jungle this is!" exclaimed Sophie. "I'm getting scratched all over."

"There are midges here too," said Katie, slapping one off her face. "We'll get bitten to bits!"

The woods they had to wade through seemed more like jungle than ever after half an hour's slow going. And then Nick suddenly spied a path.

"Here's a way through!" he shouted. "Not much more than a rabbit track, but a path that people have used at some time. Come on, we'll go more quickly now."

The woods grew less thick after that and although the path wasn't much of a path, still it helped as a "guide to somewhere", as Katie said.

They came out at last into a tiny lane, and walked down it, dirty, torn, and bleeding from a hundred scratches. Not a cottage was in sight.

"We may be miles and miles from anywhere," groaned Nick. "This is awful, like a nightmare."

"We're probably a long way from the nearest village," said Katie. "There weren't any marked on the map on this side of Brinkin Hill."

The lane finally turned into a rutted road that ran along between hedges so high that the children couldn't see over the tops of them. Then Katie pointed out something that cheered them up.

"Telegraph poles," she said. "Look, over there."

They made for the telegraph poles and came out on a road, not a main road but certainly a tarmacked road which, after the overgrown paths and narrow hedged lanes they had been following, seemed a wonderful sight.

And then they saw a farm-cart pulled by a tractor, the young driver looking half asleep in the hot August sunshine.

The children hailed him. "Hey! Can we have a lift? Where's the nearest telephone?"

The youth looked at them in surprise and disgust. "You clear off, you urchins!" he said.

"Oh, bother!" said Nick. "I suppose we do look rather awful. Come on. We'll follow the telephone wires, they must lead to somewhere!"

They walked on, tired now and very hot.

"I think I'm hallucinating," said David gloomily. "I keep imagining I can see a village in the distance with a shop that sells lemonade."

"You must be," answered Sophie. "There are only fields and trees and telegraph poles."

"Don't mention lemonade," groaned Nick. "I'm so thirsty I can barely swallow."

"I'm dreaming of a very, very large ice cream," said Katie, wiping drops of sweat off her forehead.

Suddenly, a car came round the next bend. All four children waved and signalled to the driver to stop. But he ignored them and drove straight on.

They looked at each other despairingly. Surely someone would help them?

CHAPTER 24

SAFE AT LAST

The very next person they met was a country policeman, cycling slowly along, looking extremely hot. He eyed the children suspiciously as he came near.

"Constable!" called Nick urgently. "Can we speak to you? We've some news."

The policeman heard the desperation in Nick's voice and took note of his unspeakably dirty and torn clothes. He jumped off his bicycle, looking suddenly interested. He had a big red face, a large moustache and twinkling eyes.

"Got news, have you?" he said. "What kind of news, now, would it be?"

But before they could answer, he had pitched his bicycle against the hedge and had caught Sophie and David suddenly by the arms. They looked at him, alarmed.

"You the Gathergood kids?" asked the policeman in a voice trembling with excitement. "Redheads, both of you, and alike as peas! Is your name Gathergood?"

"Yes," said David in amazement, trying to wriggle away. "How did you know?"

The policeman let go of David's arm and took a rolled-up newspaper from his inside pocket. He flipped it open and there, on the front page, to the children's intense surprise, was a photograph of David and Sophie.

Underneath there was a long paragraph. It began:

MISSING TWINS

Sophie and David Gathergood have been missing for some days now, and are feared to have been kidnapped.

They have striking red hair, and can be recognised easily . . .

"See?" said the policeman triumphantly. "I always carry pictures of missing folk about with me, just in case, you know, but you're the first I've ever spotted. You come straight along with me now. We'll go to police headquarters in Wareham."

This was all very sudden and exciting. It

was also a great relief to have a competent and sensible grown-up in charge of affairs again. However nice it was to be on their own, there always came a time when grown-ups were much the best people to take charge of things.

The policeman called for help over his radio. A car would come and pick them up shortly, he said.

They didn't have long to wait, and they were much relieved that they didn't have to walk any further. At the police station they took it in turns to tell their story to three interested policemen – the one they had first met, and two others.

One of these was an inspector, a grave-faced man who hardly interrupted at all.

Out it all came: Miss Twisley, Brinkin Towers, the locking-up of David and Sophie, then the coming of Nick and Katie, and the escape to the island, the sinking of the boat, and the long days of waiting, the visit of the strange little man at night, and the hunt for him the next day by the four men, and finally their own escape in the boat belonging to their captors!

When Nick came to this bit, the

inspector suddenly sat up very straight. He reached for a telephone as he shot out a sharp question.

"Those men are still there, on the island, did you say? My word, it's incredible! We must get going quickly on this!" He spoke rapidly into the telephone and then hurried out of the room with the second policeman.

The red-faced policeman who had found the children took them to his house nearby. His wife exclaimed in horror when she saw the state they were in.

"You need a bath and a thorough scrubbing! I never saw such ragamuffins in all my life!"

"We're too scratched and bitten to scrub ourselves," protested Sophie.

The policeman's wife, laughing, paid no attention and took them to the bathroom.

"Your clothes are torn and filthy," she said. "What will your mothers say to you?"

"Please could we use your phone?" asked Katie. "We haven't been able to talk to anyone for the last few days. Our neighbour and our mother might be starting to worry about us."

Sophie and David went up for a bath

while the policeman's wife took Nick and Katie to the telephone. They called Mrs Hall first. She was delighted to know that they were coming home for supper and bringing the twins with them. She also had some news for them.

"Your aunt is much better," she told them. "And your mother's found someone to be with her and is on her way back here. Don't try to phone her at the moment because she'll be in the car, but she's hoping to be here by suppertime."

Very pleased, Nick and Katie ran upstairs to join the twins. A little while later, the four children came down, clean and with their clothes brushed. The policeman popped his head round the door. He looked extremely pleased with himself.

"Inspector says, could you give these kids something to eat?" he said. "Things are humming! My word, this is a day!"

It certainly was. While the children were eating sausages, chips and baked beans provided by the policeman's cheerful wife, a lot was happening elsewhere.

CHAPTER 25

IT'S ALL OVER

Police appeared at the great gates of Brinkin Towers and surrounded the grounds. As no one opened the gates, they were forced open. Then, warily and cautiously, the police moved in on the house.

There were five people there, including the large woman. They were all frightened out of their lives and protested that they had no idea where their bosses were.

"Don't worry. We know all right," said the inspector grimly. "Search the place, boys. We want that ruby!"

That was another thing the children had learned with much surprise: the Rajah's Ruby had been stolen. They put together the bits they heard, and the bits they knew, and decided that the little fellow called Amar had been told to steal the ruby and he had done so.

"But instead of going back to them with

it, he kept it himself," said Nick. "And so they came after him. He may have been going to hide in the temple, if we hadn't scared him off with David's sneeze!"

"I wouldn't mind if the ruby was never found," said Sophie. "Who wants a thing like that? We don't! We don't even want our great-aunt's money. We want to earn our own."

"Well, you can always give your money away," said Katie. "You could give it to poor old people, and children with no parents, or for saving elephants or the rainforests . . ."

"We'd never be allowed to," said Sophie gloomily.

"I wonder if they've captured those men on the island?" said Nick. He didn't have to wonder long, for soon the news came through that all four men had been found hiding in the temple, and had given themselves up with hardly a struggle.

"And now they'll have to explain why they kidnapped two nice young redheads like you," said the policeman, beaming at the twins. "In fact, they'll have to answer a whole lot of awkward questions, including one they say they can't answer, and that's where they've hidden the Rajah's Ruby."

"They don't know where it is," said Nick. "It was hidden by Amar, the short Indian who came to the temple the night before we left. He knows where it is."

"We haven't found him, worse luck," said the big policeman. "He's out of the country already, likely enough. We'll never know where that ruby is, I reckon."

There was silence. Then Nick said something so remarkable that everyone stared in astonishment.

"Well, I know where it is," he said.

"You don't!" cried the others, amazed.

"I do," said Nick. "I bet you anything I do!"

"Where?" demanded Sophie.

"Do you remember the biggest statue in that little room where Amar was wailing and chanting last night?" said Nick. "Do you remember it had eyes of red stones, and we saw that they didn't match? Well, I'm sure one of those eyes must be the Rajah's Ruby, hidden there by Amar! I saw him touch the forehead of the statue and I bet he was taking out the ruby eye that was there and putting your ruby in instead!

That's why the eyes didn't match."

There was a pause as everyone digested this astonishing idea. Then Sophie clapped Nick on the back.

"You're right! I'm sure you're right!" she said. "It *was* the ruby! And I guess it was the one in the figure's right eye, too. I thought that one was surprisingly lovely."

"Well, I'll be jiggered," said the policeman, in a voice hoarse with excitement. "I must go and telephone the inspector. He'll send some one across to the island again, to see if you're right. Well, I'll be jiggered, this beats all!"

Nick was quite right. The Rajah's Ruby was found pressed into the right eye-socket

of the biggest statue, just as the boy had guessed.

The policeman drove the children to Swanage, where Mrs Hall was waiting for them. She couldn't believe her eyes when they rolled up in a police car.

"It's all right, ma'am, they've done nothing wrong," said the policeman, seeing the look on her face. "In fact they're responsible for us being able to round up a gang of crooks – dangerous thieves and kidnappers!"

He drove off, leaving Mrs Hall staring after him in amazement.

Mrs Hall turned to the children. "Well, I'm pleased to see you again, Sophie and David, but I can't imagine what you've all been up to!" she said. "Your mother will be home soon, Nick and Katie, so let's get supper ready for her and then you can tell us both what's been happening."

Nick and Katie's mother arrived back as Mrs Hall was taking supper out of the oven. The children ran to greet her and to help her in with her luggage.

"Oh, it's lovely to see you, Mum," said Katie, giving her a hug. "So many things have happened and we thought we might not see you again for weeks!"

"We've had a very exciting adventure," said Nick. "It all began—"

"Well, before you go any further, can you tell me why you didn't phone me today or yesterday?" asked their mother. "Surely Miss Twisley would have let you use the phone in the house?"

"Miss Twisley was one of the people who helped to kidnap Sophie and me," explained David, "and Katie and Nick rescued us."

"Then we were prisoners on the island because our boat sank in the thunderstorm and we couldn't call for help," added Sophie.

"Nick and Katie, I can see that you met the twins, camped out on an island with them and brought them back to Swanage," said their mother. "Did you know before you took your camping things over there that they were being held prisoner?"

"Yes, Mum," replied Nick. "But we had to try and rescue them ourselves, because if we told you or the police and the kidnappers heard the police coming, they would have taken the twins away and we might never have been able to save them."

"Nick, Katie, you could have got yourselves and the twins into a desperately dangerous situation," said their mother gravely. "Please promise me that you will always tell me all the facts before you run off on another adventure."

"Don't be cross with them, Mrs Terry," begged Sophie. "They probably saved our lives, and Nick found the stolen ruby – thought we don't really want it."

"All right, you awful children," said Mrs Terry, smiling. "Let's have supper now, and you can tell Mrs Hall and me everything that happened right from the beginning."

Later that evening, the inspector brought the ruby over to Swanage to show them, and for the first time David and Sophie saw their great treasure.

It lay in a box full of cottonwool, a deep red ruby with a strange glowing heart. They all gazed at it, dumbstruck.

"You're beautiful," said Sophie, at last. "But you're very sinister too. Don't bring bad luck to us, please, because when we grow up, we're going to sell you, and use the money to do some good and worthwhile things. Do you hear me, Rajah's Ruby?"

The ruby glowed like fire. Nick laughed. "It's done one good thing already," he said. "It's given us all a great adventure."

"Yes, and it's giving us a wonderful holiday, too!" said David. He and Sophie had been invited by Mrs Terry to spend the rest of the holidays with her and her children. "There are two more weeks to go, and we're going to spend them here! Good old ruby!"

"Looked at it enough?" said the inspector. "Well, it's going off to the bank now, and if it's ever stolen again, I'll have to ask for your help, Nick."

"You can have it!" said Nick, watching the ruby being wrapped up very carefully. "Wow, these last days have been as good as any story in a book. What an adventure!"

C. G. JUNG

C(arl) G(ustav) Jung was born in 1875 in Switzerland. Educated in Basel and Zurich, he received his medical degree in 1900 and began his career as psychiatrist in the same year at the University of Zurich. Later he studied under Pierre Janet in Paris and collaborated in clinical work with Eugen Bleuler in Zurich. He met Sigmund Freud in 1907 and for a time edited Bleuler's and Freud's Jahrbuch für psychologische und pathologische Forschungen. *Dr. Jung was the author of numerous articles and books. His Collected Works are in the process of being published in the Bollingen Series. He died in 1961.*